PRAISE FOR

Necklace of Kisses

"*Necklace of Kisses* is the most lustrous gem in the necklace of Weetzie Bat stories. I read it on the plane and had to hide my tears from the woman seated next to me." —John Cameron Mitchell

"Francesca Lia Block's writing is part of the 'fabulist' literature that's particular to Los Angeles [and] is the only American fiction that's really worth reading." —Alan Rifkin, *Los Angeles Times*

"Block's fairy tale of personal transformation succeeds as a great summer read—a fizzy cocktail of Joseph Campbell, *Sex and the City*, and Gabriel García Márquez, filtered through the blunt-edged poetry of rock lyrics. *Necklace of Kisses* is a welcome reminder that midlife is still ripe for magic." —*Time Out* (New York)

"Block uses the fairy-tale motif as a vehicle to convey the tangled-up truths that girls face on the road to becoming women. Through Weetzie and other characters, [Block] explores both societal and personal fears surrounding sexuality, power, food, death, drugs, love, creativity, depression, and loneliness in ways that are as inspiring as they are transgressive." —*Bust* magazine

"*Necklace of Kisses* offers Weetzie a chance to come to terms with who she was and who she has become, and the result is a heartfelt work of adult fantasy that sings in many voices. . . . *Necklace of Kisses* also reinforces what a lyrical but economical writer Block is." —Salon.com, a "Best Book" of the summer

"A great read." —*People*

"Weetzie's many fans will most appreciate this reunion . . . but those just meeting Block's whimsical entourage and sparkling prose will also appreciate the book's message: that magic can be found in stolen moments and, in Dirk's words, though 'love is a dangerous angel,' it's well worth the risk." —*Publishers Weekly* (starred review)

"The self-parody is as wonderful as ever—Weetzie doesn't have to save the world; she can just go shopping—and, as always, the magic is in the detail: wearing her raspberry snakeskin sandals, dipping her roll in olive oil and basil, surreal stuff happens. . . . The celebration of the silly and the magical in a scary, sad world will appeal to all those once-teen fans who remember Weetzie and, just like her, now need a rewrite." —*Booklist*

"Lovely language and ambitious ideas." —*Kirkus Reviews*

"With vivid imagery, Block has conjured another enchanting and lyrically surreal journey of love and self-discovery." —*Library Journal*

"The punk-rock loving, thrift-store dressing denizen of Los Angeles' West Side is back among the colorful, smog-filtered sunsets and brightly painted boulevards that have long inspired the muse of her creator." —Associated Press

About the Author

FRANCESCA LIA BLOCK is the author of the *Los Angeles Times* bestsellers *Guarding the Moon, The Rose and the Beast, Violet & Claire,* and *Dangerous Angels: The Weetzie Bat Books,* as well as *I Was a Teenage Fairy, Girl Goddess #9, The Hanged Man, Echo,* and *Nymph.* Her work has been translated into seven languages. She lives in Los Angeles.

Necklace of Kisses

a novel

francesca
lia block

HARPER

NEW YORK • LONDON • TORONTO • SYDNEY

HARPER

A hardcover edition of this book was published in 2005 by HarperCollins Publishers.

HarperCollins books may be purchased for educational, business, or sales promotional use. For information please write: Special Markets Department, Harper-Collins Publishers, 10 East 53rd Street, New York, NY 10022.

FIRST HARPER PAPERBACK PUBLISHED 2006.

Designed by Jaime Putorti

The Library of Congress has catalogued the hardcover edition as follows:

Block, Francesca Lia.
    Necklace of kisses : a novel / Francesca Lia Block.—1st ed.
        p.   cm.
    ISBN 0-06-077751-6
        1. Hotels—Fiction. 2. Runaway wives—Fiction. 3. Middle-aged women—
    Fiction. 4. Psychological fiction. I. Title

PS3552.L617N43 2005
813'.54—dc22   2004059651

ISBN-10: 0-06-077752-4 (pbk.)
ISBN-13: 978-0-06-077752-4 (pbk.)

06 07 08 09 10 ❖/RRD 10 9 8 7 6 5 4 3 2 1

To Lydia

Acknowledgments

I would like to thank my family, my longtime editor and beloved friend Joanna Cotler, and my current editor, Alison Callahan, for helping this book come into existence. And thanks to Charlotte Zolotow for starting it all.

Necklace of Kisses

Kisses

Where were the kisses? Weetzie Bat wondered.

Even after almost twenty years, Weetzie and her secret agent lover man still threw each other against walls, climbed up each other's bodies like ladders, and attacked each other's mouths as if they were performing resuscitation. The kisses had been earthquakes, shattering every glass object in a room. They had been thunderstorms, wiping out electricity so that candles had to be lit; then, those kisses extinguished the candle flames. They had been rainstorms on the driest, thirstiest desert days, causing camellias, hydrangeas, agapanthus, and azaleas to bloom in the garden. Those kisses, Weetzie remembered—they had been explosions.

Now there were no kisses at all.

Weetzie dressed in a pair of cropped, zippered, pale orange pants, a silver-studded black belt, a pair of high-heeled ankle-strap sandals, a black silk-and-lace camisole, a white satin trench, a pink Hello Kitty watch, and a pair of oversized rimless pink glasses with her name written in rhinestones on the lens. Then, carefully, thoughtfully, one by one, Weetzie took out of her closet:

> *a lime green, pink, and orange kimono-print string bikini she had made herself*
> *two fresh, unopened packs of men's extra-small white tank tops from the surplus store*
> *new-fallen-snowy-white Levi's 501 jeans*
> *men's black silk gabardine trousers from the Salvation Army, tailored to fit*
> *a pair of orange suede old-school trainers with white stripes*
> *orange-leather, silver-studded slides*
> *some bikini underwear and bras in black, white, pink, lime green, and orange*
> *a pink-and-green Pucci tunic from her best friend Dirk's Grandma Fifi*

Weetzie put everything into a small white suitcase covered with pink roses and fastened with gold hardware. It was very important that everything was just right—fabulous, actually. She'd read an article in a fashion magazine, "Aceness at Any Age," and realized that she had already zipped through her twenties and thirties—only ten short years each—wearing Salvation Army finery mixed with her own wacky creations. She liked the jacket made of stuffed-animal pelts and the necklace of plastic baby dolls, but at forty she wasn't sure that either looked particularly ace. And there was less and less time left to be fabulous now.

Why was fabulousness important? The world was a scary, sad place and adornment was one of the only ways she knew to make herself and the people around her forget their troubles. That was why she had opened her store almost five years ago. Everyone who entered the little square white house with miniature Corinthian columns, cherub statues, and French windows seemed to leave carrying armloads of newly handmade and spruced-up recycled vintage clothing, humming sixties girl-group songs, seventies glam and punk, eighties New Wave one-hit wonders, or nineties grunge, doing silly dances, and not caring what anyone thought.

Weetzie loved the old dresses she found and sold, because they had their own secret histories. She always wondered where, when, and how they had been worn. What they had seen. Old dresses were like old ladies. Except that the Pucci tunic, Emilia, still shone like a young girl.

In her white purse, Weetzie put her tiny pink Hello Kitty wallet, her huge black sunglasses case, a toothbrush, toothpaste and floss, deodorant, a bottle of jasmine-and-gardenia perfume, a tube of pink lipstick, a heart-shaped powder compact, travel-size bottles of sunscreen, moisturizer, hair gel, and shaving cream, a razor, a comb, and her cell phone. She smacked on some pink lip gloss and dumped that in, too. Then she went to look at Max, who was asleep with a newspaper covering his face.

Who was he? she wondered. This man with his head in a newspaper all the time. This man who had been her secret agent lover for so long and was now just Max. They had hardly said a word to each other in days. There was nothing left to say. There were no kisses or even the ghosts of kisses floating through the air, waiting to be caught.

Weetzie caught a glimpse of herself in the heart-shaped mirror as she walked out of the door of the cottage where she and Max had been together for over two decades. Her hair was short and bleached platinum blonde, as it had been since she was a teenager. Her nose, chin, and ears were pointy, as a petulant fairy's, but her mouth was wide, soft, and affectionate. Her eyes were hidden under pink sunglasses, so she could not see the little lines that revealed her age, or the tears that were not there.

Gray

When Max woke up, he noticed that the room looked different. The walls, which Weetzie had painted to look like they were sleeping inside a rose, were gray, the color of newsprint. He just kept staring at the walls, wondering how this could be, if he was still dreaming. Then he felt an aching emptiness deep in his intestines and he knew she was gone.

He went and checked the closet for her small suitcase and her pink-and-green silk dress, but he already knew they weren't there. He remembered one of Weetzie's favorite movie scenes: Grace Kelly in *Rear Window*, how she comes to see Jimmy Stewart with only the tiniest case, and everything she needs—nightgown, robe, and slippers—tucked neatly inside. Weetzie had learned how to pack like that over the years. He wondered if he had told her how much he appreciated it. When they met, she jumbled everything into large

5

vinyl shopping bags. "I'm such a bag lady!" she laughed. He had actually loved that about her, too, at the time.

Max sat down on the floor and picked up the phone. He dialed Dirk and Duck.

"She's gone," he said when Dirk answered.

Dirk was quiet for a moment. "What did you expect, man," he finally said. Then, as if realizing how harsh he sounded, he added, "Sorry."

Max said, "Do you know where she went?"

"She didn't tell me."

"The room is gray."

"It's what?"

"Gray. The walls. It's like a newspaper in here."

"You must like that."

"Not necessary."

"If we hear anything, I'll let you know, okay?"

Max started to cough. It sounded like his old smoker's hack, but he'd quit years ago. He could almost taste the nicotine now. Maybe he could go down to the liquor store . . .

"Can we make you dinner?" Dirk asked.

"No thanks, man."

"You're okay?"

"Yeah."

"Well, call if you need anything," Dirk said to the dial tone.

Instead of buying cigarettes, Max went and sat on the floor in Weetzie's closet. When they moved back to the cottage, they had converted one of the bedrooms into a closet for her because she said that ever since she was a kid, she didn't care how small her house was, as long as she could have a walk-in. He realized that he hadn't noticed what she wore in a long time. It used to be such a source of delight to him, every morning, to see how she put her outfits together. Now he ran his hands along the carefully organized racks. They were sorted by color and style, as well as chronologically. It was like looking at a little movie of their lives. There was the red satin minidress she wore on their first date with those rhinestone chandelier earrings that brushed her shoulders. The sundress made out of kids' sheets printed with piglets. The pink velour minidress. The Levi's with intricate layers of colorful suede fringe sewn down the legs. The black steel-toed engineer boots she wore with fifties taffeta prom dresses when she slammed in the pit at punk gigs.

Then he saw the pink-and-black Chanel suit she had inherited from Dirk's Grandma Fifi. He held it in his hands and felt the soft, nubby fabric. It smelled like gardenias and jasmine. She liked to wear the jacket with jeans or over a pink silk slip, the skirt with a black camisole, bare legs and stilettos. He was so relieved that Coco, as she called it, was here. It meant that somehow, maybe, she would be back.

The Lost Kiss

Weetzie had gone to her high school prom at the pink hotel. She had asked Dirk McDonald, who was the coolest of all the boys and still one of her best friends in the whole world, but at the time he told her there was no way he would ever do anything related to high school unless it was absolutely mandatory. He said she could join him for a Pink's hot dog and a gig at the Whiskey. But she was determined to experience one normal high school thing before she left forever, so when Zane Starling asked her to the prom, she said yes.

Zane Starling and Weetzie met in their social studies class, where they worked together on a project about teenage suicide. He was six foot two, with spiky blond hair, green eyes, and golden skin. In the afternoons, Weetzie roller-skated through Hollywood to his small stucco house surrounded by generations of transplanted Christmas trees. They sat in his dark, pine-scented room talking about what would make someone want to kill himself. These conversations proved how sensitive Zane Starling was, as well as perfect-looking. He told Weetzie that he had had a huge crush on her friend, Tracy Calla, but that she was an ice princess and that he was over her, which showed that he was a person of substance. He played David Bowie albums, which demonstrated that, unlike ninety-five percent of the boys at Weetzie's high school who only listened to heavy metal, he was utterly cool. Then he asked Weetzie if he could paint her, which proved that he was also artistic and attentive.

On prom night, Zane Starling, wearing a rented black tuxedo and an aqua blue shirt, borrowed his father's station wagon and picked Weetzie up. He told her she looked beautiful in the aqua blue satin taffeta dress that she had found at a vintage shop and shortened to the top of her thighs by removing two tiers of ruffles, the devilishly pointed paler aqua blue satin pumps, tiny white fishnet gloves, and an aqua-blue-rhinestone-studded cat collar. Zane Starling pinned a white-tea-rose-and-lily-of-the-valley corsage onto Weetzie's dress and handed her a present wrapped awkwardly in tissue. It was the painting he had made, and it looked just like her.

When they arrived at the hotel, Zane left the car with the valet, took Weetzie's arm, and walked her up the staircase into the ballroom, where they danced all night until Zane Starling's aqua blue shirt was soaked sheer with sweat. Then they slipped out into the gardens of the hotel, under a rose arbor, beside a small pond full of waterlilies. Weetzie imagined that Zane Starling's kiss could have healed anyone who might have thought they wanted to die, that she would see angels with shocks of iridescent hair and luminous thunderbolts on their faces. But instead of waiting to see if this was true, she pulled away from Zane Starling and told him she wanted to go home. When he dropped her off at her door, she couldn't stop crying, though she could not have said why. Later, she realized it was because Zane Starling could have been the one, and she was too afraid and too young for him to be the one, and she knew it would never happen that way again. Also, Weetzie was thinking of Tracy Calla, who was dark-skinned, had big breasts and long, shiny hair, and had sat at the table next to Weetzie and Zane Starling with her boyfriend, a model who looked at least five years older than anyone else at the prom. Weetzie kept glancing over at their table and wondering how Zane Starling could like her if he really wanted Tracy Calla. When she saw the painting he made of her, she realized even more clearly that she looked nothing like his dark, voluptuous dream girl.

So Weetzie never returned Zane Starling's call. Later, she found out that Dirk was gay. She met Max, who was small and dark and brooding, and whom she loved in all the chambers of her heart but never kissed anymore. Many nights, lying beside him, their bodies not touching, Weetzie dreamed of a pink palace full of dancing ghosts. And so she would go to the hotel now, seeking the kiss she had lost.

The Pink Hotel

The rumor behind the pink hotel was this: it was built in the twenties by an eccentric movie mogul as a palace for his fiancée, Daisy. Just before they were about to move in, Daisy suddenly died. The producer disappeared into the suites on the top floor, and the rest of the palace became living quarters for the most beautiful and desirable Hollywood prostitutes. It was taken over in the fifties by the son of the madam, who reinvented it as a hotel. Rumor had it that he performed pagan rituals on the grounds and hid statues of goddesses and horned fertility deities in the gardens. It was also said that Daisy still haunted the rooms.

You drove up a circular road, lined with palm trees and bougainvillea plants, to the pink hotel's green-glass doors. You entered a lobby with pale green carpeting, pink velvet chairs, and cream damask sofas. You took a large flight of stairs up into a grand ballroom with a pink-and-green parquet floor. On the floors above this were the rooms and suites whose walls could not talk but might possibly wake you in the middle of the night with a song.

To the left of the lobby was a gleaming-white restaurant that opened onto a terrace overlooking the main lawn. Beyond the restaurant was the bar—a separate building with a glass dome that lit up with constellations. On the right side of the lobby was a beauty salon with blue mirrored walls painted with pink cherry blossoms and gold branches. Along the back wall of the hotel was a row of shops that had originally been an atrium. A reflecting pool ran the length of the shops. Jacarandas and willow trees lined its banks, wild parrots flashing their feathers among their leaves; swans glided and flamingos posed beside the lily pads.

Any hotel exit took you down winding paths, among beds of roses, gardenias, and topiary animals, through tiny groves of citrus trees, under grape arbors and past mossy grottos with splashing fountains. The main path led you to the garden rooms—tiny individual cottages that had first been built to house the help. Beyond these was the Olympic-sized pool. At the other edge of the lawn was a Japanese restaurant and traditional gardens that had been built by the next owner, a businessman from Tokyo whom no one had ever seen but who was said to visit once a year dressed up as an actress, a trophy wife, or a geisha.

The current owner was even more mysterious.

As Weetzie left her 1965 mint-green Thunderbird with a valet who looked like Rudolph Valentino and walked through the front doors, she thought: Oh Pink Hotel, if I could be a place, you are the place I would be.

14

The Blue Lady

Weetzie went up to the check-in desk carrying her suitcase and her white purse. She took off her pink rhinestone sunglasses and put them on the pale green marble counter. A very tall, slender woman with her hair worn in an elegant chignon on top of her head stepped out from behind a small potted orange tree.

"Oh," Weetzie said.

"May I help you?" the woman asked in a soft, resonant voice.

"I'm sorry, you're so . . ."

"Blue?" the woman said.

Weetzie said, "Beautiful!"

"And blue," the woman said. She was an astonishing shade of cobalt. "Isn't it funny how no one says what they see? I don't mind. I know that I'm blue. Are you here to check in?"

"Yes," said Weetzie. "Sorry."

"No problem."

Weetzie thought of how direct the woman had been and decided to ask the question that was on her mind.

"Why, I mean how did you . . ."

"Turn blue?" the woman said.

Weetzie nodded.

"I left my boyfriend to come here," the blue woman said, gesturing around the lobby of the hotel with its domed, pale blue ceiling painted with cherubs and rose garlands. "And then I started missing him. When I called him to see if I could come home, he said he had met someone else."

Weetzie suddenly imagined Max lying in bed under his newspaper. In the vision, there was another pair of legs beside his—a woman's. Her head was covered with a newspaper, too, but she had lovely feet with purple toenail polish.

Weetzie looked blankly at the blue lady, wondering if she had somehow guessed why Weetzie was here. Then she realized that the story was a response to the question about the woman's coloring.

"And you turned . . ."

"Blue," the woman said, checking her computer. "Yes. Now, would you like a garden room or something in the main building?"

"A garden room," Weetzie murmured, looking at the plain gold band Max had given her, wondering how she could ever possibly carry off cobalt coloring.

Room Service

Weetzie's room had French doors that opened onto a tiny patio with a fountain and potted jasmine and gardenia plants. The ceiling was painted pale sky blue, the carpet was pale grass green, and the walls were papered with an old-fashioned pattern of pink cabbage roses, light purple irises, green leaves, and pale yellow stripes. There was a seashell-shaped love seat upholstered in rose velvet, and a desk and chair of pale yellow wood, handpainted with leaves and the small roses you could make by dabbing a brush in two colors of paint about eight times each. There was a big, comfortable bed with a pink comforter. The satin sheets felt like water and smelled like lavender. There was also a small refrigerator and a mini-bar. Weetzie opened the refrigerator and took out a bottle of tonic water and a bottle of grapefruit juice, which she mixed in a glass on the ice she had retrieved in a silver bucket from the humming machine down the walkway. As she put a Milky

Way bar into the freezer for later, she vowed that she would go easy on the refreshments in the room. They cost a fortune, and the money she had saved from the store wouldn't last forever. Not that she would be here forever, she told herself. And then wondered when she was planning on leaving. This question had not even occurred to her when she came here.

Weetzie took off her shoes, pulled the bedspread off the bed (she always remembered how she changed her children's diapers on those things, when they were babies), and lay down with her drink. From the room, you could hear the splashing sounds of the pool and smell the chlorine mixed with the flowers. You could hear birds in the trees and the cleaning lady whistling as she wheeled her cart down the walkway. The cocktail Weetzie was drinking bit her mouth pleasantly. Was it the quinine from the tonic water? What was quinine, anyway? Some kind of bitter salt? Weetzie finished the drink and took off her clothes. Then she went into the bathroom and filled the tub, dumping the entire contents of the hotel's green bath gel bottle under the stream. She opened the window so she could smell the garden and eased herself into the bathtub. Then she hummed "Smells Like Teen Spirit" while she shaved her legs and underarms and used a pumice stone on the calluses on her feet. She realized that she didn't have any significant songs after Kurt Cobain shot himself. It made her feel old, but there was nothing she could do about it; listening to new music hurt too much.

When she got out of the tub, she wrapped herself in one of the thick white towels that smelled of fresh-baked cake, and sat on the bed. She realized, smelling the towel, that she was starving, so she did her second favorite hotel thing to do—after taking a bath. She called room service.

"Room service. May I help you?" a man's voice said.

"I was wondering if you might have any items from the breakfast menu at this time of day?" Weetzie asked.

"I'm sorry, miss. We only have the Afternoon Snack menu available now. Until four-thirty, when we have the Pre-Supper menu available. Then we have the Early Supper menu. At six-thirty we have the Dinner Proper menu. Until nine-thirty. Then we have the Late Dinner menu. From eleven until twelve-thirty we have the Late Late Dinner menu. Then we have a Snack menu until two. From two to six we have the Wee Hour Snack. We have a Breakfast menu from six until eleven."

"What if I wanted to get eggs and oatmeal and fruit and a bran muffin?" Weetzie said. She would have been very impatient with his speech, but she liked his voice and the way he called her "miss."

"Well, we only have eggs on the Breakfast menu, and on Sundays we have them on the Brunch menu. We have fruit on the Snack menu. We have muffins and oatmeal on the Breakfast menu but not on the Brunch menu."

"Do you think you might have one piece of fruit lying around?" Weetzie asked.

"Let me look and call you back," the voice said.

Weetzie thanked him and hung up. There was something so magical about room service. You just pressed a button and talked to a nice person and then this food appeared at your door on a silver tray with white linen and ice water tinkling in a glass.

She got up and put on the TV. At home she would never do such a thing, not in the middle of a balmy, sunny afternoon. Max had the TV news on all the time lately, but Weetzie hated it. Now she put on IFC and saw they were showing her favorite cross-dresser rock musical, *Hedwig and the Angry Inch*. She realized, happily, that she loved all the songs from that show, and they were recent! I'm not so old after all, she thought. She sang *"I put on my makeup"* along with Hedwig, and danced around the room. She got out her lipstick, dabbed some on her lips, and patted her nose with powder.

The phone rang. For a second, her heart leaped, as if in expectation. What could she be expecting? It was only room service.

"I found some oats, grapes, and a kiwi," he said.

"Oh, I like grapes and kiwi! I had a dog once who loved kiwis."

"Really, what kind?"

"Are there different types of kiwis?"

"Oh, I mean the dog."

"He was a dachshund," she said, and immediately felt a lump in her throat thinking of her beloved boy. He had died in her arms at fifteen, fat and happy, but she still regretted that she hadn't wished to give him a human life span when she had the chance.

"Those dogs are so cool. I had them growing up."

"Really?"

"What was his name?"

"Slinkster Dog."

"Great name. Ours were Shirley, Keith, Laurie, and Danny."

"What about Mr. Kincaid?"

They laughed.

"You don't sound old enough for the Partridge family," she said.

"Reruns . . . Well, I better get you your kiwi."

"Thank you," Weetzie said.

"But that isn't much protein."

"I won't even ask if you have any tofu."

"No, sorry. We have plain yogurt, though."

"Oh, what the hell," Weetzie said. "I'm kind of lactose intolerant but you only live once."

They laughed again.

"Coming right up," said room service.

A few minutes later, there was a knock on the door. Weetzie was so involved with Hedwig that she had forgotten to get dressed. She put on the terry-cloth robe that also smelled like a cake, and answered the door.

Mr. Room Service looked like a faun who had escaped the Arcadian woods for the big city. He was wearing a white shirt, black pants, heavy black shoes, a white apron, and carrying a silver tray with a bunch of red and green grapes arranged elegantly beside a carefully skinned and sliced kiwi. There was a bowl of oatmeal and three small white china carafes, one with yogurt, one with raisins, and one with brown sugar. There was ice water in a glass and white tea roses in a vase.

The man grinned. "Where would you like this?" he asked.

"Oh, the bed is fine," Weetzie mumbled.

"Is it?" He winked at her as he put the tray down. "Enjoy," he said. He had that kind of lascivious mouth that looked as if it would be very adept at kissing. His eyes, though, were kind and not at all devouring.

Weetzie signed the bill, adding a generous tip.

"What brings you here, Weetzie?" he asked in a soft voice, as if he was afraid someone might hear him fraternizing with a guest. But his grin said he didn't care that much.

"Midlife crisis."

"What makes you think you'll only live until you're fifty?"

"What?"

"You said midlife. You look about twenty-five."

"Very charming. I bet you're an actor in your spare time."

He shook his head and looked at her innocently.

"Are you sure?"

"Well, not a working one."

"Who is?"

He squinted at her and then up at the Independent Film Channel playing behind her.

"You look familiar. Were you ever . . ."

"Just some crazy indie stuff with my family."

"Where are they now?" He looked around the room as if for signs of them. All he saw, Weetzie realized, was her suitcase, her white purse, her sunglasses, and her stilettos.

"My babies are off at school," she said. "I thought I'd go on an adventure."

"School? You mean boarding school."

"Berkeley and Santa Barbara," she said. "U.C. My God."

"Well, you look amazing, Weetzie. You must have had them when you were one yourself."

This reminded her of something Max had said, a long time ago, when she told him she wanted to have a baby, and she glanced down at her hands. Before getting in the tub, she had removed the ring she wore and put it in a water glass by the bed. She had never taken it off before.

Her stomach made a loud growling sound and she put her hand there, embarrassed. "Oh, excuse me, I'm hungrier than I thought."

"You better eat then. Call me if you need Pre-Supper or Early Supper or Dinner. Then I'm off. But tomorrow night you can call me for the Wee Hour Snack, Weetzie."

"Thank you," she said. "Oh, I didn't get your name."

"Pan."

Pan? As he trotted off down the garden walk, she imagined that there might be tiny horns buried in his thick curls, cloven hooves in his shoes, and, perhaps, a frisky tail in his trousers. In fact, she truly believed she saw it peeking up there above his belt, trying to escape. Room service, indeed, she thought. Weetzie, you really had better behave yourself.

The Pool

Weetzie finished her Post Lunch Late Breakfast Snack sitting cross-legged on the bed, watching Hedwig. Afterwards, she put on her sunscreen, her bikini, and her orange sandals, and trotted to the pool.

As she slid into the Jacuzzi bubbles, she realized that if she could spend all her life in warm water, she might never get upset. Whenever she needed to have a serious talk with Max, she insisted on taking a bubble bath with him. He had stopped doing this, so they just didn't talk anymore.

Try not to think about him, she told herself.

The Olympic-size pool was paved with pink, green, and white tiles and surrounded by tiled fountains, palm trees, bougainvillea plants, urns of gardenias, and tables with green umbrellas. No one else was around except for one couple reclining on chaise lounges, drinking Perrier and soaking up the sunshine. The man looked about sixty—bald, tan, with white chest hair and diamond rings on his fingers. The woman was a living Barbie doll, even down to her surreal measurements. After a while, she stood up, and Weetzie watched her wobble awkwardly on her long legs to the edge of the pool. When she dove into the water, she was strikingly graceful, swimming like a giant buxom fish through the water. She swirled and somersaulted in an elaborate water ballet, barely coming up for air. When she finally got out of the water, she was smiling radiantly. She wobbled over to Weetzie and slipped into the Jacuzzi beside her.

Weetzie felt a little uncomfortable at such close proximity to the woman's huge Barbie doll breasts. She tried not to stare at them.

"Hi," the woman said sweetly.

"Hi."

"I'm Shelley."

"I'm Weetzie."

"Where are you from?"

"I live in town. How about you?"

"We live here," the woman said. "In the hotel."

"That must be pretty glamorous."

The woman shrugged. "I come from the ocean. I miss it a lot."

"Santa Monica or Malibu?"

"Oh, just all over. Just the ocean. Sal is a producer, so he likes to be near the studios. He likes to be near the action. What does your husband do?"

Weetzie looked at her blankly.

"Or is it your boyfriend? Is he in the industry?"

Weetzie remembered that she had put Max's ring back on her finger, but she still didn't quite get the question.

"He's a director."

"He must be pretty successful."

"He does all right," Weetzie said. "But this is on my dime. I'm an independent woman."

"Oh, honey," Shelley said sympathetically, "we've got to get him in line. A man has to take care of his possessions." She reached under the water, took Weetzie's French-pedicured foot in her hands, and began massaging it.

Before Weetzie could say anything, Sal, who had been making his way over, lumbered down the steps and dunked himself into the water. "I hope I'm not interrupting anything," he said.

"Honey, this is Weetzie. Isn't that a cute name?"

Weetzie, realizing her foot was still being caressed, pulled it quickly away.

"I'm Sal," the man said. He winked at her. Weetzie wondered if she had imagined it, what with the bright sun on the pool and his diamonds and all. It all seemed like too much of a cliché.

"What do you do, Weetzie?"

"I own a shop."

"She's an independent woman," Shelley said, as if she were talking about a life-threatening disease.

Sal clucked. "Where's your guy?"

"At home," Weetzie said. "I'm taking a little vacation."

"Well, at least join us for a drink," said Sal.

Shelley nodded, shaking out her long, blond hair. For the

first time, Weetzie realized that it had green tints, maybe from a bad dye job or too much chlorine.

"That would be nice," Weetzie said. After all, she had come here for an adventure.

Weetzie went back to her room, showered, and slipped into Emilia. Then she put on her sandals and walked along the garden path to Sal and Shelley's suite in the main building of the pink hotel.

The couches were shaped like giant gold-and-rose velvet seashells. There were dimly lit fish tanks filled with exotic tropical fish swimming among miniature sunken ships and gold treasure chests overflowing with strands of pearls and jewels. On every surface were small china mermaid figurines. Shelley showed them off, one by one, telling Weetzie their names in a soft, serious voice. "Kelpie, Lisette, Pamela." The little mermaid statues looked sad, so fragile and breakable with their painted-on smiles.

"Sometimes I write little notes and put them inside," Shelley said. "I pretend I am sending them to my mother."

Sal handed Weetzie a large Sapporo. She didn't usually drink anymore, but the way the moisture beaded on the cold brown glass bottle made her mouth water and she took it.

"Sushi?" Shelley asked, holding out a tray. "Sashimi?" She daintily picked up a huge slab of raw tuna and slid the whole thing down her throat in one shocking swallow.

"It's really fresh," Sal said. "Caught it myself." He patted Shelley's rear end.

Weetzie shook her head. "No thanks."

But by the end of the evening, and after three beers, she had eaten some yellowtail, slurped a salty, jiggling, orange sea urchin, and even rigorously chewed a piece of white-and-purple octopus, just like when she was young and omnivorous.

At one point, while Sal was out of the room, Shelley leaned over and asked, "Have you ever had any plastic surgery?"

"Excuse me?" Weetzie said.

"It's just that I assume everybody does, you know. All the girls, anyway."

"I've wondered about Botox," Weetzie admitted. "But I think it is pretty gross. I can't bring myself to really inject botulism or cow toxins or whatever it is into my face."

Shelley looked at her blankly. Then she said, "Sal made me get a lot."

"He made you?"

"Well, when we met, I couldn't really get around. I mean, not on land. So we did some advanced techniques of plastic surgery and then some laser surgery and, well, this is what happened." She patted her thighs, but Weetzie was looking at her breasts.

"Those are real," Shelley said. "Do you think Pamela Anderson's are real?"

"I don't know."

"I love Pamela Anderson," said Shelley. "She's an animal rights activist and she doesn't care what anyone thinks and she had her children naturally, at home with a *doula*."

Weetzie nodded. She sort of agreed. "You look like her," she said.

"Really? But there is no way she had all the work done that I have!"

Sal came back from the kitchen with a bottle of Moët and poured three glasses. "Is she telling you her crazy stories again?"

Weetzie, drunk from the Sapporos, kept trying to remember the rhyme, *Beer on top of wine is . . . wine on top of beer is fine?* No, that wasn't it.

"Sal," said Shelley, "what's the problem, sweetie? You say yourself that everyone gets something done in this town."

"But how many other mermaids have you met at this hotel?" he asked her, winking at Weetzie and handing her the glass of champagne.

"I keep looking for them," said Shelley wistfully. "I'd love to meet them. Do you know any, Weetzie?"

Weetzie shook her head, trying to figure out what to say next.

Sal shrugged. "Welcome to La La Land," he said. "Anything can happen." He put on some cheesy disco music from the seventies, lay on one of the couches, and watched the women.

Shelley was pinning a PETA button onto the strap of her silk camisole. She looked up at Weetzie and smiled proudly like a preschooler playing dress-up. Then she leaned over and whispered, "I really am a mermaid, you know. Or I was one anyway."

Weetzie looked into her sad eyes. She whispered back, "I believe you."

"It might help if you kiss me."

Shelley smiled again and dabbed her lips with the tip of her tongue.

Weetzie realized she had not kissed anybody in a very long time. She wondered if you could forget how. She wondered how her kiss could possibly help Shelley.

The mermaid's lips tasted like salt water. As they pressed against Weetzie's lips, she felt a surge engulfing her.

She was under water, tangled in seaweed, swimming with schools of iridescent fish through dim, wet, deafening silence. A woman who resembled Shelley, but older, lay on a coral reef, weeping as she pried open oyster shells with her hands. Instead of legs, the woman's torso sloped into the thick, scaly tail of a fish. Before she could go to the mermaid, Weetzie was lifted, up toward the surface. Her head felt as if it would burst with the pressure. Then she splashed into a bright twinkling and the cry of seagulls. There was a sharp hook of pain in her hips and groin and a splatter of blood. A thick arm and hand covered with white hair reached out.

Weetzie heard Shelley gasp.

"How did you do that?" she asked.

"What?" asked Sal eagerly. "What did she do?"

Weetzie was going to say that she didn't do anything; sometimes her kisses were just strange that way, they took her places. They took Max places, too, but she had never thought too much about it. The only other people she had ever kissed—really kissed—were her best friends, Dirk and Duck, when they all made love to try to have a baby. She was going to say something, at least to try to answer Shelley's question, but didn't—there was something hard and cool in her mouth. She spit it out into her hand—a large

31

baroque pearl. Shelley saw and quickly closed Weetzie's fingers over it.

"Maybe you should go now," she whispered.

Weetzie was too astonished to do anything except get up, find her bag, mumble a quick good-bye, and leave.

There was a delicate mist hanging over the gardens, just like on her prom night so long ago. She could smell the night-blooming jasmine, the gardenias, and hear the splash of fountains and the chirping crickets. Phosphorescent green lights, hidden in the foliage, illuminated the pathway that wound back to her room.

A chill started at the nape of her neck and slid down her spine to just above the band of her underpants. It was cool now, but the chill wasn't from that. There were footsteps behind her. Were there? She walked faster, without looking back, her stilettos ticking louder and louder as she went. She reached for her key inside the white leather purse and fitted it between her knuckles.

When she got to her door, she was panting. Her hands shook as she jabbed the key at the lock. When she was inside, she switched on all the lights, bolted the door, and collapsed on the bed. Outside, the gardens were completely silent. Even the crickets and fountains held their breath.

Silly, she told herself. This is probably the safest place you could be. The cleaning lady had come in to turn down the bed, leave fresh towels, and put a pink chocolate box on the pillow.

But the creepy feeling lingered like the memory of fingers along Weetzie's vertebrae.

She untied the gold ribbons on the box and ate the chocolates. Then she fell asleep in her clothes, lights on, the mermaid's pearl still clutched in her hand.

Witch

Max sat on the floor in Weetzie's closet for a long time. He touched different items of clothing, remembering places they had gone and things she had said. The zippered leather jacket she wore when they rode his motorcycle to the pier for the first time was the color of the cotton candy they ate while they rode the carousel. "Think pink!" she had said. The sleeveless sweater covered with opalescent sequins and the cream-lace miniskirt she wore on his twenty-eighth birthday made her look like Marilyn to him. He could hear her singing "Happy Birthday" in a breathy imitation of her screen idol. Each memory made him want a cigarette. Finally he realized that if he didn't do something, he would go straight to the liquor store, buy a pack, and spend the rest of the evening in a cloud of smoke and self-loathing.

He hadn't noticed that night had fallen while he was in the closet. He hadn't eaten anything, but he wasn't really hungry. If Weetzie were here, she would have said he'd better eat, because his stomach might not feel empty but his nerves were going to be as raw as sashimi in about a minute. Still, he couldn't bring himself to even think about food. If he opened the refrigerator and saw a plate of her soy cheese green chile enchiladas covered with edible orange nasturtium blossoms, he knew he would lose it. And if he didn't see something she had left for him . . . that would be even worse.

He went outside and got on his motorcycle. He had no awareness of the air on his skin, or the scents in the wind. He could have been dressed from head to toe in black leather.

Max drove past the Chinese Theater, where Weetzie used to go to worship Marilyn's footprints in the cement. He looked up and saw the HOLLYWOOD sign, where he and Weetzie had hiked the night she tried to convince him to have a baby. Even then, he had been afraid of bringing a child into the world. As grateful as he was for Cherokee, and his witch baby, Lily, he knew that now he could never have been convinced. Not after the thing he saw on TV almost two years ago. Not after those people leaping out of the windows as the planes crashed through the two towers.

He drove past the row of all-night Thai restaurants with their strings of Christmas lights and shrines decorated with fake flowers. He saw giant neon cocktails buzzing in the air; the club where Weetzie had forced him to swing-dance in a zoot suit during her rockabilly phase; the small white shop with neatly manicured hedges and rose bushes in front. He wished he could go inside and look at the dresses hanging there in the moonlight.

He ended up at a tiny bar where he used to go with Weet-zie for drinks now and then. On her thirtieth birthday, she had worn a leopard-print silk slip and go-go danced in a gold cage, but tonight no one was dancing. He ordered a whiskey as a re-ward for not buying cigarettes. It burned his mouth like gaso-line, and he wondered what made him think he could take something so strong. All he drank now was an occasional beer.

What if she comes and finds me? he thought to himself. What if she was just hiding, waiting to see how I'd react, whether I'd pass the test? She will come up to me and touch my arm and tell me that she just wanted to know that I would miss her if she left. Just like that time when Duck left Dirk and then they found each other in a bar in San Francisco. Magic was always happening.

Someone touched his arm and he jumped. His heart slammed in his throat. He turned and saw a woman. She was about forty, slender, with short, blond hair. Even though he knew this wasn't Weetzie, part of his brain, soaked in whiskey, kept trying to believe it was.

"Max," the woman said.

"Do I know you?"

"Oh, please. I haven't changed that much, have I? Just the hair color. It's a wig. But I knew you always preferred blondes, as gentlemen do."

He patted his pockets, reflexively, for a pack of cigarettes. He could feel the carcinogenic burn already.

"Did she finally leave you?" the woman asked.

His whole body tensed as if she had slapped him. "Who the hell are you?"

"Oh, come on. I know it was ages ago, but still."

Of course he knew it was Vixanne. He just couldn't really accept that he had run into her on this night, just when Weetzie was gone. That wasn't the kind of magic he wanted. Vixanne didn't look that much different from the night Max had slept with her. Her face was harder, though.

"Leave me alone," he said.

"Then you do remember."

Max got up and pushed his way toward the door.

He knew, without looking, that Vixanne Wigg was following him.

Heaven

Weetzie woke late in the morning, took a long, hot bath with a whole new bottle of bath gel that the cleaning lady had left by the freshly scrubbed tub, and shaved her legs and underarms, nicking her ankle with the razor. After she had dried off with the fresh towels and put a Band-Aid on the cut, she called room service. Glancing at the clock, she saw it was three minutes past eleven.

"Am I too late for breakfast?" she asked.

"Look outside your door," said Pan.

She put on her robe and peeked out. It was hard to imagine that she had felt afraid here. The sun was making the hotel look pinker than ever, the jacaranda trees were filled with wild parrots. A red-haired woman in a black bikini, a black beaded choker, and high-heeled black sandals with three buckled ankle straps was walking along, holding the hand of her red-headed toddler, laughing.

On Weetzie's doorstep was a silver tray. She brought it inside and took off the heavy silver cover. There were slices of honeydew, cantaloupe, watermelon, pineapple, mango; there were blueberries, blackberries, strawberries, and grapes. There was also a huge oat-bran muffin as big as a cake, two perfectly poached eggs, oatmeal, freshly squeezed orange juice, and yellow tea roses in a vase.

She picked up the receiver. "Thank you," she said.

"I hope it's all right."

"It's perfect."

"Well, enjoy."

Something was glowing in the light that streamed through the windows, and she saw it was the pearl from last night. She picked it up and held it to the window. It was heavy and cool. It looked like the real thing, although she knew more about rhinestones from the fifties than precious stones.

"Hello?"

"Oh, thank you, I will."

"And may I recommend, there's an amazing performer at the bar tonight. The early show isn't so packed. Her name is Heaven."

"That sounds divine."

"Okay, enjoy."

He hung up and Weetzie ate her breakfast very slowly, closing her eyes to see if she could distinguish the tastes of the different fruits, rolling the berries on her tongue, comparing their size and tang. At home, she always rushed through everything. When her girls were babies, she had gotten into the habit of swallowing whole meals without chewing.

After she'd eaten, she decided to call Ping and check on the store. Ping was her best friend and a designer, and Weetzie could never have opened the store without her help, let alone escape on an adventure. She also had the best hair in the world and could always make you feel good about yours.

"Weetzie's," Ping sang into the receiver.

"It's me."

"Hi, honey-honey, how's it going?"

"Great. I'm having so much fun. I wish you could stay with me."

"Don't tempt me."

"You could come for lunch tomorrow."

"That sounds good. Hey, we sold the Chanel."

"You're kidding, that's great."

"And the silver Peter Fox platforms."

"Cool. Of course, now I want the Chanel."

"You always do."

They laughed. Then Weetzie said, "Has he called?"

"Of course," Ping said. "He called first thing. He keeps bugging me to tell him where you are."

"You didn't, did you?"

"Of course not, girlfriend. But he sounds pretty desperate."

"I don't want to talk about it," Weetzie said.

"You asked me. Anyway, we've got a customer and Hilda's daydreaming again. I'll come tomorrow?"

"Meet me at the front desk. We'll have lunch by the pool."

They blew kisses at each other and hung up. Desperate,

Weetzie thought, that wasn't what she'd expected. Depressed, maybe, but he hadn't felt desperately about her in years.

She noticed that while she was talking to Ping, she had received a message on her cell phone, though she hadn't heard it ring. For a moment she thought, Max! She had almost left the cell at home so she wouldn't have to go through this. But when she listened to the message, a voice she did not recognize, and whose gender she could not determine, said, "Where are you? Please come home. We're all so worried. Please come home." Weetzie shivered in the warm air, though she didn't know why.

She put on her bathing suit and sunscreen and went to sit at the edge of the pool, dangling her feet in the water. No one was there except the woman in the black bikini and her son. They were splashing around, giggling uncontrollably. The woman had green eyes and the reddest hair Weetzie had ever seen. Her son kept reaching up to tug on it. He had a sweet, impish face and a very small, fragile-looking body.

Weetzie remembered how happy she had been when her children were that age. She called them her little vampires, sucking her dry, and she was almost always tired, but there was something wonderful about being needed that much. Sometimes she discovered cuts and bruises on her body that she had no recollection of getting; her own pain was insignificant then. Being a mother could make you brave out of necessity. Now she was acutely aware of the tiny razor cut on her ankle, how the chlorine from the pool made it sting.

What if I had a baby now? Weetzie thought. But it would

have to be an immaculate conception; Max would never agree to it.

When the woman and her son left, Weetzie dove into the water. She came up through the spangled blue, remembering the mermaid's kiss. She wondered if Max felt the things she did when she kissed him. They had never really talked about it. After they had watched those exploding twin buildings, he never pressed his lips to hers. Maybe he was afraid that even her love could not erase those images, even for a moment. Maybe he did not want to find out that this was true.

Weetzie went back to her room and fell asleep. When she woke, it was evening. The soft, warm light stretched across the room like a tabby cat. Weetzie stretched with it, wiggling her toes until she shivered with pleasure. She couldn't remember the last time she'd taken an afternoon nap followed by a long stretch. She realized that she hadn't eaten much, but she wasn't really hungry after her raw-fish binge.

Then she heard the frozen Milky Way singing to her. It had a voice like Barry White. Not that it was something she normally ate, but she was on vacation! How often was there a chocolate candy bar sitting in your freezer calling your name with sexy soul?

Weetzie ate it very slowly, washed it down with a bottle of Perrier on the ice she'd collected from the ice machine in the silver bucket, and went to the closet, trying to decide what to wear. Emilia needed to be washed, because somewhere during the course of the previous night someone had spilled beer on her. Nothing else seemed quite appropriate. Weetzie wondered if she really had underpacked. It was a great source of pride to her that she always took just the right amount of things. You had to think like Audrey Hepburn or Grace Kelly—elegant and intelligent but with a punk edge, of course. You had to ask yourself: what would Audrey do?

Just then there was a knock.

"Housekeeping."

Weetzie opened the door and looked out into the hallway. There was a cart but no sign of the cleaning lady.

"Excuse me, missus. The 'Do Not Disturb' wasn't up," a voice said.

Weetzie noticed a large feather duster floating in the air beside the cart, moving of its own accord. She jumped back.

"What?"

"I'll come back," said the voice.

Weetzie stared as the cart wheeled away by itself down the empty hallway.

She went back inside and washed her hair, putting together outfits in her head to distract her from the mystery of the invisible cleaning lady. It was just too much for her at the moment. When she got out of the shower, she put on the white satin trench over her bra and panties and belted it with the studded belt she used to wear to punk gigs twenty years ago, added her stilettos and white bag—she was set. For Heaven, she thought. And it was heavenly that she didn't have to leave the grounds of the pink hotel to swim with sushi-eating mermaids and hear a diva sing in a small glass building with a domed ceiling that lit up like the planetarium.

The stars on the ceiling were twinkling, and a deep, thrilling voice full of sadness and tenderness rose up. A spotlight found a slender figure in a long white satin dress.

Heaven's face was like a melancholy porcelain mask. Later, Weetzie would try to remember what Heaven sang, but she only had a vague impression of ballads that seemed to tell her own story. There were songs about finding your real family, even when it's not the family you are born into. Finding your family and holding hands with them and flying off into pink skies, touching down in the dark world and then joining hands and flying off again. Only people who find their true families can survive, the songs said. By the end of the show, Weetzie had cried so many tears into her ginger ale that it tasted of quinine.

She stayed sitting at her table, unable to move. Her legs were weak and her chest was still thudding under the satin. She felt as if her heart might fall out and roll away if she stood up too quickly.

Just then, a voice said, "May I join you?"

It was Heaven.

Weetzie just nodded. She couldn't speak for a while. At last she said, "Thank you."

Heaven grinned. "You looked like you were enjoying it. Or hating it so much you had to weep, but I thought I'd take a chance."

"I don't know what to say," said Weetzie. She usually chattered away when she felt like this. But then she'd never really felt like this before.

"You don't need to," Heaven said. "Your face says it all."

Weetzie asked, "Do you know me?" and Heaven answered, "I'm not doing my job if I don't make you think so."

"But the details . . ."

"Honey, the details are everything, right? You know that. A ginger ale on ice. It's really good if you put sushi ginger in the glass. A white trench belted with a studded punk number. I mean, look at the rhinestones on your toenails."

Weetzie said, "When did you see my toenails?" She slid her leg out from under the table and displayed the jewel flower on her big toe.

Heaven shrugged. "Listen," she said. "I'm having a little party in my room later. Say about midnight. I'm in the Cherub Suite." She blew Weetzie a kiss and was off in a hush of satin.

Spin the Bottle

Weetzie heard laughter streaming out of Heaven's suite. The front room was so crowded it was hard to see the décor, but Weetzie could make out pale blue wallpaper covered with chubby, winged baby angels; pink carpet; and pink-and-blue chairs with gold wings. Swinging cocktail lounge music was playing, barely audible over the laughing people. They all looked chic but somehow wacky at the same time. Maybe it was just because she had been thinking of Audrey Hepburn earlier, but Weetzie couldn't help being reminded of the party scene in *Breakfast at Tiffany's*.

Like any great hostess, Heaven appeared in an instant to guide Weetzie through the crush of bodies. She was wearing a short red-silk kimono and high-heeled sandals and drinking champagne out of a bottle.

She handed Weetzie a bottle of Perrier. "I think I noticed you weren't imbibing this evening?" Then she took her last sip of champagne and added, "When's the last time you played spin the bottle?"

"I was too scared to play in junior high," Weetzie said.

"Oh, honey, you've never played? We'd better do something about that."

Heaven clapped her hands, and immediately a group of people formed a large circle. They sat down and began chanting, "Heaven! Heaven!"

Their lovely hostess took her empty champagne bottle and put it in the middle of the circle. Then she licked her lips and spun it. The bottle wobbled and finally stopped on a very good-looking man with dark, curly hair and lascivious lips. Weetzie realized it was Pan. Heaven smiled gleefully and opened her arms wide, but before he could get up, the bottle kept turning, as if of its own volition, and stopped on Weetzie. From across the circle, Pan winked at her.

"Heaven," he mouthed.

Weetzie sat very still as Heaven turned to her.

"I've never kissed anyone so much prettier than I am before," Weetzie said. "Well, at least not until last night, I guess. There was a mermaid."

"You're pretty cute yourself," said Heaven.

Weetzie closed her eyes and felt Heaven's large, delicate hand take her own. She was still wearing Max's ring. Heaven turned it softly on Weetzie's finger.

"He misses you," she whispered into Weetzie's ear. "He is doing things like sitting in the closet and sniffing your clothes." She tsk-ed.

Weetzie felt tears behind her eyelids but she didn't open her eyes. Heaven went on, "Don't go home yet, though. Your necklace isn't finished."

Necklace? wondered Weetzie. Then she waited while Heaven leaned over and pressed her large, lovely lips to Weetzie's smaller lips.

Weetzie felt her body being lifted. She and Heaven, holding hands, rose into the air above the crowd of people and out the door of the suite into the redolent, balmy, crickety night. On their way up, palm fronds brushed roughly against their faces. The sleeves of Heaven's red kimono filled with air. Weetzie's satin trench billowed up around her, revealing her white-lace panties. Below, Weetzie saw the pink hotel as if it were an architect's model. She saw the symmetry of the gardens, the careful placement of rose bushes, ponds, and arbors. She saw the outlying rooms and the main building, the bar, the tiled pool, the Japanese restaurant.

They went on, through the night. Weetzie saw her city with its tiny, car-lined boulevards, its miniature palm trees, its jewel-box lights. She saw the club where she went to a punk gig with Dirk the first time, and the club where she danced in a go-go cage on her thirtieth birthday. The dome of the observatory where James Dean shot Rebel Without a Cause. *The battered carousel at the top of the hill in Griffith Park. Her little store with its columns and French doors. She saw trash and homeless people and fountains and limousines. She saw the cottage that had been given to her and Dirk by his Grandma Fifi when she died and where Weetzie had spent over twenty years designing clothes, raising her children, sleeping in the same bed with Max. The lights were all out. Even the TV wasn't on. Everything was so dark and quiet. Weetzie tried to turn her head to Heaven to ask if they could stop there and look in . . .*

She thought she heard Heaven's voice. "Oh. I guess he's not just sniff-ing in the closet now."

Weetzie opened her eyes and realized she had her hand in Heaven's lap, right on top of Heaven's sizeable erection. She moved it away, embarrassed.

"No problem, baby," Heaven whispered. "That was a great trip. Do you do that all the time?"

Weetzie felt something in her mouth, making it hard for her to answer. She spit out a red stone.

"It's Grandma Ruby's!" Heaven said. "For your necklace."

The Darkness
Inside

As Max got onto his motorcycle, he felt a hand on his bicep. He pulled away. Vixanne Wigg was standing in the harsh parking-lot light, staring at him with her tilted, purple crazy-looking eyes. Somewhere in the darkness beyond the parking lot, Max heard glass breaking and a man yelling.

"I told you to leave me alone," he said, but this time his voice sounded weaker.

"Just come home with me," she said. "We can just talk. I bet you have a lot on your mind."

Max turned his face away from her. He could feel her breath on his neck. It smelled like apple liqueur, sweet and harsh at the same time, intoxicating.

"Besides, we need to talk about our daughter. I haven't seen her in years. I want to know how she's doing."

Max turned the key and revved the engine of his bike.

"I promise," Vixanne said. "I won't even try to touch you. Think of all the problems that caused before!"

He drove away, leaving her on the sidewalk. The stars were like broken glass; he wondered if that was the sound he had heard, some kind of cosmic smashing. The air stank of gasoline and garbage. A mummy, bandaged in rags, was pushing a shopping cart, talking to the night. A siren screamed: "She's gone! She's gone!"

He found himself driving to Vixanne's house in the hills without even thinking. It was as if something was propelling him. When he slept with her before, and tried to explain that she had put some kind of witchy spell on him, Weetzie hadn't bought it. Not that she didn't believe in magic—that was the main thing she believed in. She just didn't think that Vixanne needed a spell. It was only Max, being weak, being hurt. Maybe she was right. Maybe he was just being weak and hurt again. But still, he couldn't stop himself.

He rode up the circular driveway and parked the bike. She was waiting for him at the door, her long body silhouetted darkly against the light of the front room. She led him inside.

Her paintings were everywhere. Witch Baby had told him about them. They rarely talked about Vixanne, but once, after Witch Baby had run away for a while, she told him what she had seen. They were all portraits of Vixanne Wigg, done in rich, glossy paints, full of fury and lush beauty. He was relieved to see them. They made her seem like a person with a heart—barbed and bleeding with thorns—instead of a hollow sorceress.

Vixanne handed Max a glass filled with greenish liquid,

which he didn't touch. But he did sit down. It was more like collapsing.

"How is the witch baby?"

"She's not a baby. You'd know that if you ever spent time with her."

"You wouldn't want that, now would you? Her *mother* wouldn't want that."

In spite of the sarcasm, he thought he heard something almost melancholy in her voice and noticed that she was looking over at a painting he hadn't noticed before—a young woman with a tangle of black hair and eyes like large purple flowers.

"She's growing up," he said. "Lily. She's at Berkeley and she's studying really hard but I think she's depressed. She still does this thing where she collects newspaper clippings of the worst shit she can find and papers the walls with them."

"Like you."

He put his head in his hands and pressed his thumbs over his eyeballs until there was a kaleidoscope of dark, broken color.

"Tell me what you see," she said.

"They say that kids thought, every time they showed it on TV, they thought it was happening again. So they had to stop showing it. But I can't turn it off."

She nodded, tapping her fingernail on the glass he didn't want.

"What else?"

"There was this documentary. They showed firefighters responding. And this one said how he was filming it but he had to turn the camera away, because there were people on fire, running. He said, 'No one should have to look at something like that.' "

"But you see it anyway," Vixanne said.

"I used to see movies everywhere. I started making movies in my head, because that was the only way I could deal with what was really going on. It always worked before."

She went over to the fireplace and stirred the dead coals. Dry ash rose up, charred remains.

"That thing that happened. It wasn't only about what happened to all those people. It was your darkness. You need to remember," Vixanne Wigg said before Max left her again.

Lunch

Ping Chong Jah-Love met Weetzie at the front desk the next day. Her hair, which was short and black as jet, had been tipped with fuchsia and lavender since the last time Weetzie had seen her. She was wearing oversized purple sunglasses, a white minidress, and white-wood platform sandals. When Weetzie saw Ping, she started to cry.

"Girlfriend!" Ping said. "What is the matter? You'll spoil your mascara."

They always joked about spoiling their eye makeup, even when they didn't have any on. Weetzie didn't laugh this time, though.

"Come on," Ping said, "let's go to the pool."

They sat under a green umbrella and ordered gazpacho, green salads, and mineral water with lime. Weetzie said, "I've been in this dream. But when I saw you, I realized that nothing has changed out there."

"I changed my hair color," Ping said.

"It's lovely," said Weetzie.

"And yours—perfect as always," Ping said. Then she touched Weetzie's hand. "Maybe this—you being here—will change him."

"It's been so extraordinary," said Weetzie. "And I never use that word! Like a magical-realist book or a Fellini movie. I haven't felt this way in about ten years."

"Well, that's good, honey. Just enjoy it."

"But what about when I come home? I don't know if I can ever come home."

"I'll have to sell a lot of Chanel to keep you here, babe. Speaking of Chanel," she added, "I brought you something."

She handed Weetzie a shiny, see-through pink-and-silver shopping bag from the store. Inside was Coco.

"I thought you might want her. I snuck in when he wasn't home."

Weetzie thought she would cry again. Now that she had the suit, she felt as if she had really left.

"Did I do the wrong thing?"

"No, Ping. Thank you."

"This doesn't mean I don't think you'll be back."

"I know."

"Weetzie, I remember how much you wanted him."

Ping and Valentine Jah-Love had been there from the beginning, when Weetzie dreamed of finding her secret agent lover man. They watched her putting on her torn, delicate dresses and stomping boots, and they told her she looked beautiful. They listened to her stories about stumbling drunkenly through nightclubs, letting boys put handcuffs on her, and they told her they were worried. They heard her laugh about her bad luck when inside she felt there was a fountain of tears trying to gush up. They tried not to act too in love in front of her, even though they could never keep their hands off of each other for very long. Then Max came, and they breathed a sigh of relief. It wasn't until just weeks ago that Weetzie told Ping about the death of kisses.

A huge blue butterfly, the size of a hand, flew onto the table. Weetzie and Ping gasped. They had grown up with small orange, white, and even black California butterflies, but never one this color or size.

"I knew this hotel was magical!"

"Either that or it's a bad sign of global warming," said Ping.

Weetzie stared at the butterfly, hard, and thought, If it lands on any part of my body, it means Max and I will stay together.

The blue butterfly rose up, circled delicately, hesitated above Weetzie's left hand, and then flitted away into the day. Weetzie sighed.

"He wants you, too, you know. He's just afraid." Ping checked her oversized white wristwatch, then leaned over and kissed Weetzie's cheek. "I'm sorry, honey, I have to get back to the shop. Will you be okay?"

Weetzie nodded, still seeking the blue wings, but the butterfly—lucky sign or dark omen—was long gone.

Monsters

After Ping left, Weetzie decided to cheer herself up with a manicure and pedicure. It was, after all, as Heaven had pointed out, all about the details. If her toes and fingers were shiny and cuticle-free, she always felt a bit brighter and lighter, even when her heart had darkened and sunken heavily into her chest.

The salon was almost empty, except for two women in white lab coats, the red-haired woman from the pool, and her son. He was holding a bottle of silver polish, which he had grabbed from the manicurist, and running in circles around a giant golden Buddha with offerings of silk lotus blossoms and glass mangoes at its feet. The boy's mother, who had one silver-tipped foot, was begging him to bring the bottle back. She was upset, Weetzie could tell, but also amused, trying not to let herself laugh and ruin the effect.

Weetzie watched this for a while and finally said, "Can anybody here help me?"

The woman looked at her, but Weetzie kept her eyes on the running boy. "I have a monster chasing me," Weetzie said.

The boy stopped. He actually seemed more concerned than Weetzie would have thought; she hoped she hadn't frightened him.

"I heard that silver nail polish keeps monsters away."

The boy looked at the bottle in his hand. He looked at his mother and his features seemed to get even smaller in his tiny face. Then he handed the manicurist the bottle, hopped up onto his mother's lap, and glared suspiciously at Weetzie with his bright, tilted, silvery little eyes.

"I'm sorry," she said. "I didn't mean to scare anybody."

The woman was wearing a pale blue silk kimono with cherry blossoms and gold branches that matched the walls of the salon. She graciously waved her wet silver fingers in the air. Her voice was silvery, too, and mysteriously accented. "I think he's all right. Are you all right then, Bean?"

"Monsters?" he said.

"There aren't really any monsters. The lady was playing a game."

He seemed satisfied with this and started to stroke his mother's hair. She mouthed a thank-you to Weetzie, who was taking off her sandals and rolling up her white jeans. She plunged her feet into the basin of warm suds and sighed. How she loved a pedicure. It was, she truly believed, one of life's great small pleasures. While one of the beauticians scrubbed, rubbed, trimmed, and polished Weetzie's toes, she glanced over at the woman and her son. They both had skin so white you could see the veins beating under it. It looked even paler, somehow, against their scarlet hair. Weetzie noticed that the boy's ears formed long, downy points at the top.

Weetzie closed her eyelids as the beautician massaged orange-blossom scented lotion into her legs and feet. When she opened her eyes again, the red-haired woman and her son had disappeared. Weetzie had the eerie feeling that, perhaps, they had never really been there.

"That other lady," she asked the beautician. "Where do you think she was from?"

"We're from Vietnam," the woman replied.

Weetzie wondered if this answer confirmed her suspicions about the redheaded hallucination.

"And what brought you to the pink hotel?" she asked, to be polite.

The woman had very broad, high cheekbones, full, beautiful lips, and large teeth.

"Our father died in the war. He was cleaning a pool the last week before the war ended and a bomb went off. Our mother had six children to take care of and no money. One day it got so bad, we're all so hungry, we had to eat a tree. I remember my brother got so sick. That was when my mother decided to find a way to get us to this country."

"How did she do it?" Weetzie asked.

"The tree told her. It told her that my sister wasn't our father's daughter."

Weetzie was still trying to understand this, when the other woman said, "I had to take a blood test." Weetzie noticed that she had the same mouth as her sister, though she was much taller and larger-boned. "I found out I have American blood."

"We hated the American man that hurt our mother," the first woman said. "But he made it possible for us to come here."

Her sister scrutinized Weetzie's face. "Why are you here?" she asked.

"I needed time away from my boyfriend," Weetzie said, feeling embarrassed at how trivial it sounded after the women's story.

"You need to show him your fingernails! He'll like how pretty you look now! Do you want a bikini wax, too?"

Weetzie started to repeat that *she* was the one who needed time away, but decided against it.

"How much is this?" she asked when her nails were pale, glossy pink, and adorned with rhinestone flowers.

"Eighty," the woman said softly.

Weetzie was used to paying sixteen dollars at one of the local nail salons—Fairy, Cute, Star, or Happy. Now she understood the Happy name.

"She paid for you," the sister said.

"Who?"

"That lady that was here."

Weetzie thought, Well, I know she's real, then. And what a nice surprise!

"You helped her."

Weetzie shrugged. She realized she hadn't really helped anyone very much since she had been here. She certainly had been helping herself, but that didn't seem to count. Especially after what the beauticians had just told her. She gave them tips the size of two Happy manicure/pedicures, eased her feet carefully into her orange slides, and left.

She saw that she had another cell phone message, though, again, she hadn't heard it ring.

It was the same androgynous voice.

"Please, please, we're all so worried. Please come home."

The red-haired woman and her son were at the pool that afternoon. The woman, wearing a black bathing suit that was held together with lots of silver hardware, was trying to apply sunscreen to her wiggly son's white-white skin.

"Thank you for my nails!" Weetzie said.

"Oh, you're quite welcome. It's the least I could do. I would have had to go around with five naked toes!"

"But it was so generous. I had no idea how much they charge here. I could have gotten about five of those for the same price at Happy Nails."

"Where is that?" the woman asked. "Is that where you are escaping from?"

"Escaping?"

"Stay still, Bean!" the woman cried as her son began to hop in circles around her. "I thought that everyone who stays at a hotel is escaping something. Or someone, I suppose."

"I'm just here to relax," Weetzie said quickly.

The woman smeared the last of the sunscreen onto the tip of Bean's nose; she took off her sandals, took his hand, and they splashed into the pool. Weetzie came and sat on the tiled edge, swinging her legs, dipping her toes.

"Where are you from?" Weetzie asked.

"We're escaping," Bean said. He took a breath, dove underwater, and then came back up, shaking his head like a wet Irish setter pup, drenching Weetzie. "From the monsters."

"Really," she said. "Then there really are monsters?"

"When Bean was born, my family tried to take him away," the woman said. "They have this horrid baby-stealing tradition. They take their own kin and substitute them for someone's newborn. It's just brutal."

Weetzie, who never in her life had been short on things to say, realized that it was happening quite a lot lately.

"We've been all over. This place is especially lovely, though. But it is cutting into Uncle Red's inheritance. Along with all the dominatrix clothes I got in Italy!"

"Can I buy you dinner tonight?" Weetzie asked. "To make up for the nails?"

"We don't really go out after dark."

"Monsters," Bean added.

"Breakfast then?"

"That sounds lovely."

Weetzie's head was spinning from the sunshine on the water and all the talk of stolen babies. She mumbled something about meeting on the terrace at ten. She started to walk away but the woman called after her, "We don't know your name yet."

"I'm Weetzie Bat."

"Peri," the woman said. "Good to meet you."

"Be careful of the monsters!" Bean shouted before he plunged into the pool.

Esmeralda

When Weetzie returned to her room, the door was open and she saw the cleaning cart in the hallway. She tiptoed up and peeked inside. The feather duster was hard at work, flicking through the air by itself.

"Excuse me," Weetzie said, coming inside.

"Yes, missus, sorry. I'll be done in a minute," replied the voice.

"Do you mind explaining this to me," Weetzie said. "It's all seeming a little too surreal at the moment."

The duster stopped moving and the door of the room swung closed. Weetzie backed away.

"Don't be scared, please."

"Then please tell me what's going on. Believe me, I know this isn't an ordinary hotel."

"No," the voice said. "That's why I come here. And people

told me I was good because people don't want to see you too much."

"You're invisible?" Weetzie said.

"Yes. I come from El Salvador. I was a secretary there, for an executive. My grandma taught me how to make myself invisible, to keep safe. But one time, I tried to not be invisible anymore and it didn't work. I stayed invisible. So I came here. It was easy to come here and get a job like this, so I don't mind it so much now. I'm so sorry if I scared you."

"No," Weetzie said. "No, that's fine. I just wanted to understand. What is your name?"

"Esmeralda."

"Hi, Esmeralda. I'm Weetzie."

"Hello, Missus Weetzie."

"I love the fresh towels and shower gel and how you turn down the bed and leave chocolates on the pillow. Thank you so much."

"You're welcome."

Weetzie watched the door open and the cart wheel out of the room and down the hall.

"I'll see you later," she said, before she remembered that she probably wouldn't.

Angel

That night, Weetzie put on a freshly laundered Emilia with her white jeans and black sandals and took the red lacquer bridge over the koi pond to the Japanese restaurant. The fish glowed orange, red, and black under the surface of the water; their movements made her dizzy. She was still feeling light-headed and needed a nice, grounding meal, she told herself. Since she'd been here, she had hardly touched her diet staples, at least not her current ones. When she was eighteen, she could have lived on raw fish, chocolate, and beer, but not anymore.

She sat at a quiet table surrounded by red and white cat statues with one paw raised, as if swiping at prey, and wiped her hands with the warm washcloth that the very tall, surprisingly broad-shouldered Japanese waitress brought. Then Weetzie ordered miso soup, spinach with sesame, edamame, sautéed pumpkin, rice balls with umeboshi plum, cold soba noodles with scallions, and tofu steak. Each item came in its own small red, black, or terra-cotta bowl or dish; she ate slowly with her chopsticks. Almost immediately her headache went away.

While she was trying to decide if she could stuff another thing into her mouth, a gentleman approached her table. Weetzie rarely saw men she would describe this way, but he was the real thing.

"Excuse me," he said, "I'm sorry to disturb you, but my friend and I thought we recognized you. Were you in *Dangerous Angels*?"

Weetzie laughed. "That was so long ago!"

"My friend, Sable, is a huge fan. He has a picture of you on his Web site."

Weetzie glanced over to his table, where a young, blond Kurt Cobain look-alike with a goatee and glasses was hunched over his rice bowl. He smiled shyly at her.

"Would you care to join us?" the gentleman asked.

Weetzie thought, A true adventurer must always accept the invitation.

The blond, it turned out, was Tristan Sable, an actor who played an angel on a popular soap opera. The gentleman was his producer, Dashell Hart. Sable, he said, had recently introduced him to Weetzie and Max's work.

Sable smiled shyly. "He's like the new Cassavetes."

"And that makes you Gena Rowlands, darling," said Dashell.

Weetzie sighed. "I wish. She's a—"

"Goddess," they all said at once, rolling their eyes skyward, and laughed.

"Are you working on anything new?" Sable asked.

"I'm working on my store," Weetzie said. "I have a store. Max is working on discovering how depressed the news can make one man."

Sable and Dashell nodded sympathetically. "And that's why you're here?"

Weetzie shrugged. "I'm not sure why I'm here, exactly. I wanted an adventure. Or something. A rewrite. I had my high school prom in this hotel."

They all grimaced.

"At least you went," Sable said. "Did you go, Dashell?"

"Heavens no! I was so shy I couldn't even have asked any-one to sit next to me in the cafeteria."

"Me either," Sable said. He looked at Weetzie. "In high school, I had a puppet named Stem. He was a lamb, I guess, but I never really thought of him as a lamb. He was just Stem. I carried him around with me everywhere. If I really got upset, I'd have to have Stem communicate for me."

"Prom-king material," Dashell said gently.

"Exactly. I was really desirable."

"Look at you now, darling," said Dashell.

"And you play an angel," said Weetzie. "How cool is that?"

Sable shrugged ironically. "Have you seen the show?"

"I think it's an unsung masterpiece, if I do say so myself," Dashell said. "In its way. A bit kooky, though. All these vam-pires and witches and things we make him battle."

Sable said, "I really like how you met the witch in *Danger-ous Angels*. That Jayne Mansfield fan club coven. How did he come up with that?"

"It all happened," Weetzie said. "Basically."

"And how Witch Baby came," he said. "That was amazing."

Weetzie smiled. But she was thinking about Max sleeping with Vixanne Wigg, who gave birth to Witch Baby and left her on their doorstep. Weetzie hadn't really thought about that in years. It was easier to consider the witch baby, Lily, as her own daughter. Suddenly her stomach cramped up, just like the first time Vixanne had come to the door. Maybe it was nothing; she had just eaten too many rice balls?

"Do you enjoy producing?" Weetzie asked Dashell, to change the subject.

"Let's put it this way, as my mother used to say, it's better than a stick in the eye." He chuckled.

Weetzie said, "My dad worked in the industry. It was a love-hate thing. Do you know Charlie Bat?"

"*Planet of the Mummy Men?* My God! That's kitsch of the highest order. I actually apprenticed with Irv Finegold for a while."

"You're kidding!" Weetzie wished her father were here. He would have been able to tell them his stories about how her mother, Brandy-Lynn, insisted on tailoring the mummy rags to show off her figure, how he had once seen Marilyn Monroe on a set, about the hidden Holocaust and black-list references he and Irv Finegold had worked into *Mummy Men*.

"What else did your father do?" Dashell asked.

"Nothing was made. He moved to New York and did some plays. The whole thing was really frustrating."

"I've been trying to get my penguin movie made forever," said Dashell. "Do you know much about penguins?"

Weetzie shook her head.

"They're really wonderful creatures. The males stand on the ice forever, holding the baby eggs on their feet until they hatch. Isn't that marvelous? What man would do that, I ask you? And the females go off to restore themselves. Just like you're doing, darling."

"A little late," Weetzie said. "I think I've needed this since my baby was born."

"Well, good for you. A girl's got to get away."

"This whole place is like a movie," she said. "You wouldn't believe all the strange things that keep happening."

The way they cocked their heads inquisitively and the brightness of their eyes made her think of penguins. How could she explain strange? She was glad when the waiter interrupted with the check.

"We'll have to do this again sometime," Dashell said as he kissed her cheek by the koi pond.

Weetzie hugged him. Then she hugged Tristan Sable, who felt much more muscular than he looked. She thought she noticed something odd, prickly, bunchy-crunchy under his white shirt.

The men asked if they could escort her to her room, and, at first, remembering the walk home after the mermaid's kiss, she almost said yes. But then it seemed like an imposition, so she went down the path alone after the Valentino look-alike arrived with Dashell's daffodil-yellow Jaguar.

It was later than she had realized, and, once again, the walkways were deserted. I'm not going to be afraid this time, she told herself. I'm in the safest place in the world. Of course, this was also what the blond ex-wife of a certain infamous football player must have thought when she was attacked and slain just a few miles from here. Weetzie shivered from scalp to toes.

The footsteps started the same way as before, even and precise like the ticking of a clock. Weetzie hurried under the shadows of the palm trees. There seemed to be another shadow, too, moving with her, but maybe it was just her own. Maybe the footsteps were just her own, too, echoing on the pavement. Still, she was dripping sweat and hardly breathing when she got to her door.

There was a soft crunching in the leaves outside her window, then silence. In the morning, she told herself, she would look for footprints. Now she bolted the door, switched on all the lights, found HBO on cable. Then, although she wasn't the slightest bit hungry, Weetzie called room service.

Pan

He came to the door wheeling a cart covered in linen. She had ordered fruit ices, because after the fright she'd suffered, she decided she deserved—and needed—a bit of sugar for comfort. There were six little scoops—watermelon, mango, peach, lemon, lime, and pineapple. They were decorated with wafer cookies and sprigs of mint. There was also a bottle of water, a glass of ice, a silver spoon, and pink tea roses in a vase.

"Are you all right?" Pan asked when he saw her face.

"I'm a little freaked. I thought I heard someone following me."

"Do you want me to call security?"

She shook her head. She was too embarrassed for that. "It was probably my imagination."

He nodded and handed her the bill. She signed it, adding another big tip, and when she handed it back, they looked at each other for a moment. She felt a tingling in her breasts and between her legs. It surprised her and made her curious.

"Are you having a good time?" he asked. There was something almost shy about the way he was looking at her now.

"It's amazing. Strange, though."

"How so?"

"I don't know. The people. Like tonight. Do you know who Tristan Sable is?"

"Isn't he on that soap?"

"Yes. He plays an angel. I met him and his producer tonight at dinner."

"I'd give anything for a part like that," Pan mused. Then he added, "I rented one of your films."

Weetzie laughed. Oh, God, how weird, she thought. No one had paid attention to those movies in years, and now twice in one night!

"I liked it. I'd like to talk to you more."

"Sure."

"I get off in an hour."

For a minute, she just looked at him. Her face felt hot. Then she realized he wasn't talking about getting off that way. What was she thinking?

"May I come by?" Pan asked softly. "We could watch some TV."

Weetzie nodded.

"Your dessert is melting," he said as he left.

✳ ✳ ✳

Pan came back.

"Would you like something from the bar?" she asked.

He held up his hands. "No thanks. I don't drink."

"Soda? Juice? Water?"

"I'm fine. Relax. Tell me about you."

"There's not much to tell. I have a shop with my friend Ping. We sell vintage and our own designs. I have two girls in college. I used to be in these little films my boyfriend made."

"Do you miss it?"

"Acting? Not really. I wish I could do something a little more meaningful now."

"It's meaningful to people who watch you," he said.

He told her about how the teacher asked his first-grade class what they wanted to be when they grew up. All the kids raised their hands to say teacher or fireman, and Pan's answer was "an actor on a TV show."

"Not a movie star. I wanted to be inside that little box my mother was always watching day and night. Then, when I got older, I really wanted it. I thought it would make me less of a freak."

"How were you a freak?" Weetzie asked. "You are so good-looking and charming."

"I was always so horny," he said. "I think I went through my entire adolescence with a hard-on." He laughed. "I scared all the girls off. I'd go home after school and sit in front of the TV getting high and getting off."

"What shows?"

"Oh, anything. *My So-Called Life.* Claire Danes! And bad TV. I mean, reruns like *The Bionic Woman. Welcome Back, Kotter.*

I had this fixation with *The Brady Bunch.* I thought that the reason it was so popular was this whole underlying incest theme. I mean, here are these two families of kids living together, perfectly matched up, pretending to be brother and sister. These girls with their blond hair and miniskirts."

"You liked Marcia Brady?"

"No, Jan. I liked to think about Jan and Peter."

Weetzie laughed. Then she admitted, "I liked Danny."

"Who?"

"*The Partridge Family* Danny. He was this chubby, red-haired kid—I mean, Keith was the one you were supposed to like. But I thought he was kind of hot when I was eight. He was funny."

"That's right. I told you about my dogs."

"You're almost as bad as I am."

Pan said, "I figure if a show makes me laugh, cry, or come, I have to give it credit. If it does all three . . ."

"Okay, which shows?"

"You go first."

"No, you."

"Okay," said Pan. "*Buffy the Vampire Slayer.*"

"No way."

"What?"

"That's my favorite show. I'm supposedly too old for it but I love it. And you are totally outside the demographic. What are you doing?" She playfully pushed his shoulder.

"It fits my criteria. Laugh, cry, come."

"Buffy's cute."

"She's cute, but Willow's the one for me."

Weetzie loved Willow, the shy, red-haired lesbian witch.

"I love you," Weetzie said.

"What?"

"You're kind of a geek, like me."

Pan nodded.

"I was heartbroken when that show went off the air," Weetzie said. "But it was so funny, the last episode made me so happy. I thought for sure they would kill her off at the end. I was bracing myself. Instead, here's this girl who has had this huge vampire-slaying responsibility on her shoulders her whole life and then she realizes that she's finally free, she doesn't have to save the world anymore. And now she knows she can just be a girl, finally. She can just go shopping. She can just play."

"Like you're doing here?" Pan asked.

"In a way. Not that I ever have had that much responsibility. I mean, I've had to take care of my mom, some, especially when my dad died. And I raised my kids. And Max, that's my boyfriend, he's been having a hard time since 9/11."

"Sounds like you've slayed a few vampires," Pan said gently. He twisted a ring on his finger. It had a large purple stone.

"What's that?"

"Amethyst. It means 'against intoxication.' "

He stared at Weetzie. She could feel her face getting hot again. "All kinds?"

"What?"

"Does it protect you against all intoxicants or just drinking and drugs?"

"Why?" he asked.

She looked away from him and turned on the TV with the remote. "What other shows do you like?"

"*Six Feet Under. Sex and the City.*"

"I love you more," Weetzie said lightly. "I hope you don't mind me asking, but are you gay?"

"Excuse me?"

"Only gay men and girls have such good taste."

He shook his head and gave her one of his lascivious looks. It made her breasts buzz.

"So why do you like those shows? Undertakers in Los Angeles and frustrated, fabulous female friends in Manolo Blahniks in New York."

"Laugh. Cry. Come."

"I guess it's the same criteria in any relationship," Weetzie said.

"You did those things to me in your film," said Pan.

She held his bright gaze for a longer moment. He looked just like a Roman marble of a faun, Weetzie thought. Tilted, wide-spaced eyes, high cheekbones, small, flat nose, broad mouth, cleft chin. But his skin and hair were dark and his eyes so dark brown they were almost purple, like his ring. It was hard to see the pupil, but Weetzie thought it had a slightly vertical shape, like a goat's. When he smiled, there was a gap between his smallish, very white front teeth. Weetzie remembered hearing that gap was supposed to be a sign of sensuality. She wondered if he still had those constant high school erections, but she didn't dare glance down at his pants.

"I want to make you laugh and cry and come," he growled softly.

"We can't," said Weetzie, moving away from him. She examined her manicure for flaws.

"Talk to me," he said.

"I just can't. Because of Max." She stood up. "I don't know what I'm doing even having you here. I was scared and you're so cute. I'm sorry."

He nodded, bouncing his shiny black ringlets. His skin smelled of almonds. "I'll go," he said. "No worries."

She saw that outside the sky was whitening and there was dew trembling on the leaves. The air smelled faintly of smoke. She wanted to tell Pan to come back but he was already far away, down the path.

Dirk McDonald,
Boy Detective

When Dirk got to Weetzie's, Hilda Doolittle was sitting at the counter in the sunny front room, drinking an iced mocha latte with extra whipped cream and writing poetry in her journal. She wrote, "The God in You," and then crossed it out and wrote it again. She looked up, saw Dirk standing there, and jumped, then adjusted her heavy black-framed glasses on her nose. Her boss's best friend wouldn't want to catch her slacking, especially with a name like Doolittle. There was a new shipment of good-as-new vintage punk T-shirts to sort through, and a couple of customers were drifting around the store.

"Hey, Hilda. Have you heard from Weetzie?" Dirk asked. His face looked worried.

"Nope. Ping's been working with me. I think she might be away or something?"

"Where's Ping?"

"She had a lunch date."

Just then, Ping Chong Jah-Love came walking in, swinging her lavender handbag and tottering on her platforms, like a child playing dress-up. She hugged Dirk and complimented him on his hair. It was cut very short, dyed black, and styled with lots of product, the way he always wore it now. Nothing adventuresome, like the Mohawks or rockabilly pompadours he used to sport, but he liked the attention anyway. She could still get away with fuchsia-tipped locks, he thought. Some women have that advantage over men.

"I was just asking Hilda about Weetzie," he said.

Ping gestured for him to follow her into the back room.

"I'm not supposed to tell anybody," Ping said.

Dirk couldn't help feeling hurt. Suddenly he was anybody? He had always been Weetzie's best friend, since they were practically just out of headgears. It was true that recently they hadn't been as close. Actually, maybe it was longer than he thought, ever since Weetzie and Max had moved out of the house they all shared and back into the cottage. But still Dirk didn't understand why she hadn't come to him.

It didn't take much for Ping to figure out what he was thinking.

"She had to tell me. Because of the shop. But she doesn't want Max to find out."

"I won't tell Max," Dirk said. "She knows that."

Ping noticed the box of T-shirts that Hilda Doolittle had neglected, and began to take them out. She held up a Siouxsie and the Banshees. "I wonder if this one was mine," she said.

"I know none were mine," said Dirk. "They were all ripped to shreds by 1985."

Feeling satisfied with their proven cool credentials, in spite of their age, they were able to return to their conversation.

"I promised Weetzie," Ping said.

"You just saw her, didn't you?"

Ping ignored him and waved a Cramps T-shirt in the air. "I have to go chew Hilda out for not getting these done!"

When she left, Dirk picked up the light purple faux-crocodile purse and opened it. He knew that Ping was a hopeless lady-who-lunched matchbox collector. And there it was, among the jumble of tropical-drink-garnish paper parasols, bubble gum wrappers, and exotic shades of lipstick—a gold matchbox from a certain well-known pink hotel. Dirk tossed it back in the purse and slipped out the rear of the store.

Daughters

Weetzie's night with Pan lasted until the Wee Hour Snack time, and it felt as if the minute she finally closed her eyes, she had to scrape them open again to answer the telephone. At first she denied it—her ears must be ringing with fatigue, it was the neighbor's phone, who would be calling at such an early hour?—but finally she realized it was not going to stop, and she groped for the receiver.

The Blue Lady said politely, "Good morning. This is the front desk. You have some visitors in the lobby."

Weetzie reflexively pulled the sheets over her breasts as if she had been caught in bed with a lover. She thought she could still smell Pan's almond scent on the bed linens. Who could her visitors be? Had Max found her? Her mother? Not that Brandy-Lynn would bother; she was too busy having her hair done and drinking her martinis. Whoever it was—Weetzie felt like one of the twelve dancing princesses caught, unable to attend her secret nightly ball. Was her adventure over so soon?

Actually, it was more surprising than a visit from Brandy-Lynn or Max. The guests, Blue Lady said, had announced that they were Weetzie's daughters.

Weetzie dropped the phone without returning it to the cradle. She pulled on the white tank she had been wearing the night before. The white jeans had some soy sauce on them, so she wore the black trousers with the studded belt and stuffed her feet into the orange sneakers. She didn't stop to wash her face or comb her hair.

Cherokee and Witch Baby were sitting in the lobby. When they saw her, they stood up. Their features were motionless in their faces, making them both look like little angry dolls. They didn't say anything.

"What are you doing here?" Weetzie said. "You're supposed to be at school."

"What are you doing here?" Cherokee snapped. *"You're supposed to be at home? With Dad?"*

Weetzie gestured for them to follow her out onto the terrace. It was a humid morning and she was nervous; in seconds, she was soaked with sweat. She felt like a ladyfinger that had been dunked in rum, while her daughters were chilled cucumbers, ready to be sliced for tea sandwiches. Maybe it was something about the hotel that made her think this way. The jacaranda trees were shedding purple blossoms, there was a faint scent of rain in the leaves, waiters in crisp white shirts were spreading linen cloths on the wrought-iron tables. On the lawn below the terrace, a white tent was being set up for a wedding later that afternoon. Men in white jackets were running back and forth, carrying chairs, tables, ice sculptures in the shape of swans, and urns of peonies, lilies, and white roses. It was all so elegant and perfect; she didn't want it to end.

"I needed some time," she said. "A little vacation. This is the first time I've done this in my whole life. Ever."

"But you didn't tell Dad!" Cherokee yelped. "He called us the first day. He sounded terrible!"

Weetzie wondered what terrible sounded like. She thought Max always sounded that way lately, but then maybe just when he spoke to her, not his babies.

"How did you find out, anyway?" she asked. "I told Ping not to mention anything."

"Dirk told us," said Cherokee. "And that is so adolescent of you! To not tell anyone."

"I needed some time alone," Weetzie said again. She realized how feeble it sounded. "Why are you so angry at me?"

Witch Baby spoke for the first time then. Her purple, tilted eyes flashed as brightly as the diamond stud in her nose. "Look at you," she snarled. "How old are you? Look at your outfit."

That hit Weetzie below the studded belt. "Excuse me, Lily," she said sharply. "Look at *your* outfit."

Witch Baby had on a white men's tank top, low-slung black trousers cut off below the knee, a black belt with silver studs, and orange suede sneakers. She turned away and smoothed one hand over her newly shaven head.

"And you got everything you have on out of my closet," Weetzie said to Cherokee.

Her other daughter shook out her long, blond braids. She was wearing a hot-pink satin slip over jeans and pale pink stilettos.

"Not the jeans!" said Cherokee. "They're Juicy Couture. And anyway, we're young," she added softly.

"I may not be young, but I am a cool mom and you are lucky to have me," said Weetzie. "And it is just mean for you to come here and talk to me about my fashion sense. It is just mean!"

She turned away and looked out over the hotel grounds. The palms rustled and the flowers turned up their faces with the first tiny drops of rain. The water in the pool whispered as the drops hit. The birds were silent, and there were no blue butterflies in sight. Weetzie wondered if the rain would affect the wedding ceremony, what the bride was thinking as she put on her veil, if mud would splatter her dress.

"I will come back when I'm ready," Weetzie said. "You can tell your dad that I need this time. And you both need to get back to school."

"Fine. We will."

Weetzie wanted to call them back, ask them to stay for breakfast, a swim, spend the night, maybe. They could all cuddle in the big bed, eating chocolates and watching cartoons like they used to. But she knew they wouldn't stay.

She thought of Cherokee, at three, watching Weetzie put on the gold-lace coat from Grandma Fifi. "Mommy, you look like a princess." Cherokee dressing up in Weetzie's leopard-print silk slip, fur-trimmed cream-cashmere sweater, and gold mules. "I want to look just like you." Witch Baby never said that. She was sad a lot of the time. But Weetzie knew that even her changeling daughter had wanted, in some ways, to be like her. And now they had looked at her so coolly, as if she were only monstrous in her orange sneakers.

Witch Baby

On the ride back to Berkeley, Witch Baby put down the convertible top of the black 1965 Mustang that had been her high school graduation present. Now that her head was shaved, she didn't have to worry about the nest of snarls the wind would make in her hair. She played a mix tape Weetzie had given her when she moved out, and yelled the lyrics.

"'*She had to leave . . . Los Angeles!*'"

City of people with plastic in their faces and bodies, plastic in their wallets, worshippers of plastic. She was glad to be going back to Berkeley but it made her sad, too. She lived in a co-op on the south side of the campus, near Telegraph Avenue, but she never talked to anyone there.

I'm busy studying, she told herself. That's why I don't have friends.

Her arms and back always ached from the huge anthropology books she lugged around, and her eyes stung from staying up all night, reading. Her stomach growled. She lived on huge glass goblets of coffee from her favorite café and mushuritos from the cart on campus—flour tortillas wrapped around shredded carrots and cabbage, bean sprouts, tofu, and plum sauce.

I won't be here forever, she told herself. This is just a weird rite of passage—college in America.

It helped when she thought of it as a ritual. Shave your head. Don't speak. Fast. Walk everywhere. Look straight ahead. Don't smile. Read until your eyes fall out. Do not think about the boy you have loved forever.

" 'She bought a clock on Hollywood Boulevard the day she left/It felt sad . . . ' "

She arrived in the late afternoon. The sun was filtering down through the trees along College Avenue. The air smelled of coffee beans and flower pollen. Fresh-faced students with tan, muscular legs walked along or rode their bikes. There was no one here she could call to join her for a stroll or a coffee.

She saw a pretty young girl walking along with her mother. They were dressed almost exactly alike, in Lacoste shirts, cargo pants, and sandals, and they both had blond, blunt-cut hair. Witch Baby remembered how Weetzie had driven her up here when school started. They had eaten vegetarian curry at an Indian restaurant and bought jewelry and CDs on Telegraph. Witch Baby got her ear pierced again, right on the street, at the very top of the ear, through the cartilage.

Weetzie said, "Are you sure this is what you want?" and

Witch Baby thought she meant the earring but it was about Berkeley. The homeless in People's Park, the tiny, dark room in the co-op.

"You know you can always change your mind."

Witch Baby just shook her head and taped to the wall above her bed a newspaper clipping about a young man who had been kidnapped and murdered because he was trying to save rain forests in Latin America. Being here was her rite of passage.

But sometimes she wished she had gone back with Weetzie. As much as Witch Baby told herself she hated Los Angeles, she had to admit that a part of her loved it. She loved the poisonous flowers that grew everywhere, how everyone just accepted their virulence because they were pretty. She loved what the smog did to the sky, the cruel pink streaks it made. She loved the wild animals that lived right there in the middle of the city. That was how she felt in Los Angeles, like a wild thing hiding in a canyon. Finding patches of Mexican evening primrose and creek beds and caves to hide in.

There was something else Witch Baby loved about that city, though she didn't want to admit it. It was still the place where her family lived.

Weetzie didn't seem to need to punish herself, Witch Baby thought. Weetzie was sad sometimes, but she knew how to enjoy life. She saw the colors in things. Somewhere deep inside, no matter how confused she was, Weetzie loved Weetzie. That was why she could leave Max and his newspapers and stay at the pink hotel. Watching soap operas and getting her nails done, Witch Baby thought huffily. But then again, that was what Weetzie wanted.

And what did Witch Baby want?

When she got back to her room in the co-op, she sat cross-legged on her bed and went through her mail. Her heart pounded the way it always did when she saw the post-card from Nepal.

> *Niña Bruja,*
>
> *Here my eyes are so full of beauty and sadness. I need to stop traveling for a while. I am moving back to Los Angeles, where I can work for my dad. Will you be there? Can you move back? I think I have found what I was looking for.*
>
> *Angel Juan*

Three more years, Witch Baby told herself. Three more years and then maybe you will be ready, you will have passed the test, you will be able to be with him again. Three years of living inside the big books, eating mushuritos, finding more places to punch holes in your body.

What was Angel Juan looking for? she wondered.

What am I looking for?

Cherokee

Cherokee arrived back in Santa Barbara in the blue '65 Mustang, which had been her high school graduation present, just in time to shower and change clothes for her evening shift.

It was a clear night. The sea fog hadn't come in, and the lights of the city below the hotel were like little fallen stars. Could you wish on them? Cherokee wondered. Beyond them she could see the bay. As she served pumpkin bisque and lobster ravioli she thought about her mother dining alone at a restaurant like this. A middle-aged woman in a beautiful hotel, trying to figure out what she needed. Sipping her Chardonnay, dipping her roll in olive oil and basil, patting her lips with her napkin, noticing the lipstick stain. Leaving behind her home, her lover, her babies.

But then we aren't really babies anymore, are we? Cherokee thought, even though she still felt like one sometimes.

After work, she decided to take a walk around the hotel grounds. She couldn't stay long; she knew Raphael would worry. He was home now, in their little bougainvillea-covered adobe apartment on State Street, reading his philosophy books. He'd been at class when she got home; they hadn't seen each other since she'd left for Los Angeles. She moistened her lips with her tongue, thinking of the way he tasted, his hard hands and sensitive fingerpads, the almost-girlish fullness of his mouth.

The pool was down the hill in the middle of an expanse of lawn. Cherokee imagined what it would look like from above. Whenever she went on trips as a little girl, she liked to see the Southern California pools from the airplane. They cheered up the brown landscape of Los Angeles, little spots of blue. And this city was so much prettier than L.A. She loved the tiled terra-cotta roofs on all the Spanish-style buildings, the missions and parks and roses, the cute shops filled with bright, sexy clothes, the houses in the hills with their dense gardens, the expanse of beach at the edge of the town.

Cherokee took a path that wound among the low, white wooden buildings. She passed the reflecting pool in the grape arbor, the little waterfall, the small stone that marked where someone had buried their beloved dog. Exotic plants from all over the world were planted thoughtfully, with tiny signs marking their name and place of origin. Enchanted garden. Cherokee sat on a white wooden swing and listened to its soft creak, the chirp of the crickets, the sound of a piano concerto coming from someone's room.

She knew that her grandparents, Weetzie's mother and father, had come here on their honeymoon in the fifties. It probably wasn't much different-looking then. She imagined them sitting on this swing, looking out over the gardens, holding hands. Brandy-Lynn was beautiful, a blond starlet with skin that lit up a room. Charlie was tall and thin, with a dark, chiseled face; from the pictures she'd seen, Cherokee thought he looked a lot like a stretched-out version of her own dad. Charlie had met Brandy-Lynn on the set of a movie he'd written. Supposedly, it was love at first sight, a whirlwind romance, courthouse wedding, and off to Santa Barbara. Obviously, Cherokee thought, that was before drinks thrown in faces, screaming fights, smashed vehicles. Weetzie had told her, once, about the day Charlie left. Brandy-Lynn, who never got her hair wet, dove right into the pool when he walked away. Twelve-year-old Weetzie, who was standing on the balcony of the condo, wondered for a second if she would have to save her, but Brandy-Lynn came up for air, only to jump into a martini glass and not emerge for years.

Cherokee wondered if Weetzie and Max ever fought like that. She didn't think so; she'd never seen it. But she knew things weren't right between them. Her dad always seemed so preoccupied now. He never talked about ideas for his films, he never talked about anything, really, except the news. Cherokee hadn't seen her parents acting affectionate with each other in a while. She and Witch Baby used to find it rather disgusting—all the hugs and kisses—but now she secretly watched for some signs that her parents still cared about each other.

She tried to imagine what it would be like if Raphael stopped holding her. It was impossible to imagine. They had loved each other for so long that she didn't even really know what loneliness felt like.

Maybe it wasn't fair. Why did she always receive affection when her sister seemed so hungry for it? And if someday the love stopped, what would Cherokee do? What would she do if she was forty years old, no longer sylphlike and utterly charming, possibly wrinkled, and unkissed?

I would come here, Cherokee thought. I would dine on smoked salmon, capers, and toast at the restaurant. I would swim in the pool. I would sit on this bench and listen to the crickets. I would hope that Raphael would miss me as much as he does now.

Brunch

Weetzie went back to her room and showered, scrubbing her skin vigorously with a washcloth and fragrant green gel until her eyes watered. She was determined not to cry. She put on a fresh tank top, her orange pants with the zippers, and her orange sneakers. She fastened the Hello Kitty watch around her wrist, wondering at what age she would decide she was too old to wear it. At least her sunglasses and bag were dignified, she decided as she marched back out to meet Peri and Bean for breakfast. Well, at least her bag!

It was Sunday, and there was a huge buffet brunch in the hotel restaurant. Long tables were decked with hot, covered silver serving dishes of scrambled eggs, bacon, sausage, waffles, pancakes, and French toast dusted with powdered sugar. There were fruit plates decorated with scattered pomegranate seeds, shredded coconut, and toasted pecans. There were platters of lox, cream cheese, red onions, olives, cucumbers, and tomatoes. One chef was making omelets to order with a selection of finely chopped vegetables. Another chef was making fresh crepes. There were baskets of bagels and pumpkin muffins and a whole table displaying miniature fruit tarts that looked good enough to wear. Weetzie's stomach grumbled; the stress of the morning had taken a lot out of her. She sat down to wait for Peri and sip her ice water with lemon.

She took a few pink packets of sugar and crunched the granules in her fingertips, thinking that she would take them back to her room to mix with moisturizer and use later for a facial scrub. If Charlie were here, he would make free lemonade for her, the way he used to do, adding lemon slices and sugar to the ice water.

But he would be so old now, frail. His hand would feel different. Maybe she was thinking of him because of the wedding on the lawn, the visit from her angry girls, the strange weather. Outside the glass walls of the restaurant, the rain was falling heavily, while the sun tried to peer through, tinting the air silver.

Weetzie put the sugar packets into her purse, where her fingers grazed her cell phone. She picked it up and checked—yes, there was a new message; someone had just called.

The voice sounded more desperate this time, almost frantic. "Please come home! Please, we want you to come home, now! This isn't fair. You need to get back here. Right now!"

"Hello there," Peri cried, rushing up and kissing Weetzie on both cheeks so that her high, tight braid swung and tickled Weetzie's neck. She was wearing a short, zippered, black, high-collared dress with her buckled sandals.

"You look nice."

"Thanks. I wonder if the effect is a bit too dominatrix-y? Have you been waiting long?"

"Oh, I'm in no hurry," Weetzie said. "I was just watching the rain. I wonder if it will spoil the wedding."

"There's a wedding?"

"On the main lawn. They have a tent," she said, more wistfully than she had intended.

Peri glanced at Max's ring on Weetzie's finger. "Where did you get married?" she asked, trying to wipe Bean's runny nose as he twisted away from her, toward the buffet tables. Weetzie was silent, and Peri said, quickly, "I'm not married myself. His father was an elf king from the emerald mines. Haven't seen him since. Shall we get our food?"

Weetzie followed her to the buffet, thinking about weddings. A few years ago, she and Max had gone to dinner at a vegetarian restaurant in Topanga Canyon where little white lights twinkled around the cupids in the fountain and coyotes watched from the creek bed as they exchanged rings. It was enough of a ceremony at the time, but now Weetzie wished they had done more. She had worn a narrow, white-brocade suit with big buttons on the jacket, rhinestone-studded sandals, and gardenias in her hair, but secretly she had longed for a dress in the shape of a wedding cake and a veil that touched the ground.

While she was waiting for Peri, Weetzie had carefully planned her six-course meal, but by the time she got up to the tables, she was overwhelmed and only took some sliced cucumber, fruit salad, and scrambled eggs.

"Aren't you coming?" Peri asked after she and Bean had devoured six pieces of bacon, an avocado omelet, a bagel with lox and cream cheese, and a pumpkin muffin, and were heading back for more.

"Oh, no thank you," Weetzie said. "I'm not as hungry as I thought."

When Peri and Bean came back with fruit salad, fruit tarts, and French toast, Weetzie was examining a slice of cucumber and thinking of her children. Peri touched her hand. "Are you all right, then?"

Weetzie smiled, but her eyes filled up with tears when she heard the concern in the woman's voice. She hadn't realized how much she needed to talk about what had just happened with Cherokee and Witch Baby.

"My daughters just came by."

"Here? Oh, my. I hope they're not like my family," Peri said.

"Monsters," muttered Bean as he gobbled up a slab of French toast drenched in maple syrup.

"They're angry that I left," Weetzie said.

Peri and Bean both stopped chewing and looked at her with their slanted gray eyes. They nodded sympathetically.

"I'm not ready to go home."

"You can join us," Peri said. "We might go to New Orleans next. There's a big old Victorian house in the middle of a graveyard that takes people like us in."

"I've always wanted to go there," Weetzie said. "New Orleans. But I don't think I can."

"It has a pool with selkies," Bean said. "And there's a war-lock who gives fencing lessons."

"Well, for now," Peri said, "after we eat, let's take a look at that wedding, shall we?"

Weetzie and Peri went up to the terrace to watch the guests arrive, while Bean sat at their feet, examining the ants on the blue hydrangeas. The rain was still coming down steadily, and the guests hurried over the lawn under their umbrellas. Weetzie wished she could see inside the tent. It glowed with warm light, and she could hear the musicians playing some odd, charming music.

The wedding party, dressed in pearl gray, jade green, and pink, stepped across the grass, umbrellas held low, and van-ished into the tent. After a while, two people appeared in a golf cart.

Suddenly, the rain stopped. The sun broke through, mak-ing a rainbow that arched across the tent. A young woman in a huge puff of white dress and a white veil leaped out of the cart. She lifted her skirt, and three little girls in green-and-rose-colored dresses rushed out from the petticoats, holding giant peony bouquets. The woman and the girls ran toward the tent, giggling. An older man got out of the cart and fol-lowed them, trying to catch hold of his daughter's train, which was about to drag into the puddles. Weetzie thought she saw the bride levitate just in time to avoid the muddy water and land, pristine, at the opening of the tent. She dis-appeared through the white flaps.

Weetzie looked at Peri. "That's a wedding!"

"Yes. It makes me wish the elf king stuck around," Peri said.

For the first time, Weetzie registered the elf-king thing. Before she could ask more, Peri kissed Weetzie's cheek. "Thank you so much for brunch. Let's play again sometime, before we have to rush off."

"When is that?" Weetzie asked.

"It depends on my family," Peri said breezily. Then she took a darker whisper. "I'm in the garden rooms—45A. If you see any weird, red-haired folk lurking around, do let me know, will you? I think they're getting closer. They really can't take Bean from me."

"Of course," Weetzie said. She watched Peri scoop up her son and walk away. She hoped she wouldn't have to fight any monsters. She hardly had enough energy to face her own children.

Wedding

Weetzie woke from her nap rested and saw that the rain had not returned. It was a clear, warm night. The trees were sparkling like green-glass chandeliers. Weetzie thought about the way the sun had appeared with the bride in the golf cart. It would be a story the bride could tell her children and her children's children. Weetzie wished she had a story of her own. She would have at least liked to tell Cherokee and Witch Baby about the flower girls inside the dress and the flying bride, but she knew her daughters might never forgive her for this adventure and would probably not want to hear anything about it.

Weetzie put on Coco with the back camisole and black stilettos, but instead of cheering her up as it usually did, the outfit made her more depressed. She decided to walk down to the main lawn and see if the tent was still there.

There it was, brighter in the darkness. A few stars hovered

in the sky, looking as if they wanted to come down and join the fun. The strange, whimsical music was still playing, though it sounded much wilder than during the ceremony. Weetzie tiptoed through grass still damp from the morning rain and stood at the flap of the tent.

It opened, and one of the flower girls peeked out. She had a wreath of tea roses on her blond ringlets, deep-set blue eyes, and a mouth like a rosebud with tiny, sharp teeth that showed when she smiled. She gestured for Weetzie to come inside.

"The Boom Band is playing!" she said and disappeared into the crowd. Weetzie almost turned and went back out, but no one seemed to mind that she was there. Two tall, thin brides-maids with large noses and hats like giant peonies smiled at her. An elderly gentleman tipped his top hat, revealing one long, thin strand of hair standing straight up on his head. Twelve girls with flowing hair, long brocade dresses, and con-spicuously worn-out slippers on their feet were holding hands, dancing in a row. A petite, dark-haired woman breezed past Weetzie.

"I love your suit!" she cooed.

"Thank you," said Weetzie. "I love yours!" It was the thinnest silk she had ever seen.

"Come by my shop sometime!" She handed Weetzie a tiny silk pouch. Inside was a silver card that said "Lacey's Beautiful World." Weetzie tucked it into Coco's pocket.

On a small stage, three bearded musicians in turbans were playing instruments Weetzie had never seen before, though they resembled some kind of huge, twisted horn, a sitar, and a giant xylophone with pastel keys. Everyone seemed to be dancing. A tall, skinny man with a big nose, a shaved head, and a tuxedo with tails was holding the dark-haired, gamine, puffy-dress bride. Weetzie blinked at the little smiling hearts and blue birds fluttering around their heads.

Someone was tugging on Coco's sleeve. It was the little flower girl. The band boomed. Before she knew it, Weetzie was dancing.

"Doctor Seuss!" the girl said.

"What?"

"Doctor Seuss. *Oh, the Places You'll Go!* 'You'll find the bright places where Boom Bands are playing.' "

A very tiny old lady with a lavender sari and violets in her white hair joined Weetzie and the flower girl. The woman was so graceful, like a young bride herself. Weetzie thought, That is how I want to be. She took the woman's hand and they danced and danced. People moved back to watch them.

When the song ended, the woman led Weetzie over to a table.

"Why are you here?"

"Oh, I'm sorry," said Weetzie. "That little girl brought me in. I should leave."

The woman laughed. "No, you're welcome at the wedding. I meant, what brings you to the hotel?"

Her eyes were like a saint's—clairvoyant, transparent blue against her teak-colored skin. Weetzie wanted, suddenly, to tell her everything.

"I had my prom here," Weetzie said. "There was this boy. I never kissed him. And now Max, that's my boyfriend, we've stopped kissing. We've stopped doing anything."

While she listened, the woman's fingers were moving in the air, as if she were weaving invisible threads. "He was your psychopomp," she said. "The boy."

"What's that?"

"Spirit guide. To help you find your hidden possibility. Animus. The godlike male part of you. If we meet our counterpart before we have fully developed ourselves, it can be overwhelming. Like Psyche looking at the light of Cupid, it can blind you if you aren't prepared."

The music stopped and someone shouted, "Cake!"

A cake the size of the bride's wedding dress was wheeled into the tent. It was in the shape of a white palace with turrets, balustrades, balconies, windows that glinted as if there were little lights inside, and a garden of real pinkish-white roses. Weetzie was so struck by it that she didn't notice the waiter at first. He left the cart and hurried back out, but on the way, she touched his arm.

"You get around," she said.

"I try to take every gig I can get," said Pan, winking. "What's your excuse?"

"I crashed."

"I heard it's all vegan," he said, glancing back at the cake. "Fruit-juice sweetened. I heard the bride is lactose-intolerant, too!"

He waved and disappeared through the flap in the tent.

The woman in the lavender sari smiled. The violets bobbed in her hair. "You've come to the right place, my dear," she said to Weetzie.

Escape

After she had eaten a piece of cake that looked like part of a miniature white palace, tasted like a kiss, and was certain not to give her indigestion of any kind, Weetzie left the tent and crossed the lawn. She felt dizzy from eating nothing but wedding cake for dinner. The light on the pathway was eerie and green. Her cell phone rang, and she jumped, answering without thinking.

"Child," a voice said. Weetzie realized it was the same voice that had been leaving the strange messages, but this time it sounded entirely different—hoarse, animated, deranged. "You are being punished for abusing your private parts! You bring that aberration back here this instant! Do you hear me! I know you do! Peri!"

Weetzie almost flung the phone to the ground. Instead, she began to run. Tick tick tick, went her heels. Tick tock tick tock. She reached for the key she had tucked into Coco's pocket.

She was certain she heard footsteps behind her, but this time it sounded as if they belonged to more than one person. Weetzie stepped off the path into the bushes and waited.

Three figures came along the walkway. They were all very thin, with pale, narrow faces and long, red hair; one had a long, red beard, too, but besides, and even in spite of, this it was hard to tell their genders. They were dressed in prim, dark suits, and shirts with buttoned-up collars. One was wheeling a huge, old-fashioned baby carriage. As they passed, Weetzie peered inside and saw that it was empty.

She stumbled through the bushes away from the carriage, her heels sinking in the mud from the morning rain. Coco's sleeve caught on a twig, and Weetzie heard the thread snag; every sound seemed amplified. She began to run, as fast as she could, to reach Peri's room from the other side.

The lights were off. She ran around to the French doors and knocked.

"It's me," she whispered as loudly as she could.

Peri let Weetzie into the room. If she had looked white before, now she was truly transparent. She was wearing a long, old-fashioned white-lace nightgown and white socks, and her hair streamed down over her shoulders.

Weetzie didn't have to say anything. Peri immediately woke Bean, who was sleeping on top of the covers in a dark jacket and sneakers. He sat up as if he had been expecting this. His mother slid a long, fitted black-leather trench coat over her nightgown and zipped her feet and legs into black-leather, thigh-high boots. She picked up the black-leather satchel that was standing ready by the door and took Bean in her other arm.

Then, before Peri and Bean disappeared through the French doors into the night, the red-haired woman leaned over, kissed Weetzie's cheek, and pressed something cold and hard into her palm.

There was a rapping at the front door. Weetzie crouched down under the writing desk and held her breath. After a while, the knocks grew softer and softer. Weetzie put her head on the deep, grass-colored carpet and closed her eyes.

She dreamed of a large, spiky wrought-iron gate that opened onto an old graveyard. Among the stone angels and thick, humid foliage, stood a dilapidated gingerbread house. Peri and Bean walked up the front path to the porch. In the moonless night, with their black clothes, they were almost invisible.

The front door of the house creaked open. A man stepped out.

He was tall and fine-boned, with eyes that glowed in the dark, like a cat's. His skin was stained with soot. His ears were like an animal's— pointed and covered in pale, silky fur.

He took Peri and Bean in his arms. The door closed behind them.

Weetzie saw morning creeping into the sky.

Someone was whistling.

Weetzie jumped up, bumping her head on the writing desk. The sun was streaming in through the large windows, and a feather duster was hovering in the air.

"*Hola*, Missus Weetzie," Esmeralda said. "Are you all right?"

"*Hola*, Esmeralda." Weetzie scrambled to stand. She realized she was holding something so tightly in her hand that it had almost cut the skin.

It was an emerald.

She said good-bye to Esmeralda and hurried outside. In the gardens, it was once again impossible to imagine anything even slightly sinister. But there was something strange. As Weetzie hurried out of Peri's room, in sandals caked with dried mud, she saw that someone had painted the front door a pale silver. And the old-fashioned baby carriage she had seen the night before was abandoned on the path.

She stood there, dazed by the sun. Suddenly, a man in white pants and a cap drove up in a cart and began sanding off the silver paint. Weetzie wondered how long it would take to cover an entire door with silver nail polish, especially if you were the size of a bean.

She hoped that, at least, it had worked to keep the monsters away.

Soaps and Shopping

After what had happened the night before, Weetzie was not interested in adventure, at least not for the moment. As soon as she got back to her room, she opened the windows, ate a bag of pretzels, drank some grapefruit juice from the refrigerator, took off all her clothes, took a bath, pulled down the covers, and tucked herself under the cool, fresh sheets. She closed her eyes and slept until she was awakened by the phone.

A man's voice said, "I have Dashell Hart on the line for Weetzie Bat."

"Oh, yes? Hi."

"Hi, darling," said the producer.

"How are you?"

"Fine. Listen, I hope you don't mind me calling. I've been talking with Sable and he came up with an idea for a project we'd like to discuss with you. Can you meet for lunch tomorrow at the hotel?"

Weetzie was delighted. She was starting to feel that, except for warning Peri and Bean, she hadn't been doing anything very constructive while she was here. Maybe Tristan Sable and Dashell Hart had an idea for a movie.

After she hung up, she reached for the remote and put on the TV. The soap opera, in which Tristan played an angel, was on. He looked very different, clean-shaven and without his glasses. Weetzie watched him grab the shirt collar of a depraved-looking, greasy-haired man in black-leather pants, who, she gathered, was a vampire, while she dialed room service.

She was half relieved and half disappointed when a woman answered to take her order of a vegetable platter and bottled water. But when the doorbell rang, Pan was standing there. Weetzie pulled her robe tighter around her.

"Is this all you're eating?" he asked her. "You can't survive on crudités and wedding cake, lady."

"I don't have much of an appetite. Things keep happening."

He brought the tray in and set it on the bed. "Whatcha watchin'?"

"Eden Place."

Tristan Sable was now unbuttoning the blouse of a young, slender blonde. He kissed her neck as he slid the fabric off her tan shoulders. Weetzie wondered if he ever took off his own shirt on the air, and if she had imagined the feathers pressed beneath the cotton when she hugged him the other night. She felt her face heating up once again.

"It's not bad," she told Pan, without looking at him.

"That guy's got it made," Pan said. Then he added quickly,

"To have a part like that," and she realized he didn't want her to think he was referring to Tristan kissing the actress.

"I'm having lunch with him and the producer tomorrow," Weetzie said.

Pan checked his watch. "I better get back to work."

Weetzie caught his wrist. He swiveled around to look at her. "Isn't it funny," she said, "how you keep turning up? Like wouldn't it be a kick if you happened to be working the lunch shift tomorrow?"

He winked at her.

"With a head shot and résumé?" she said as he opened the door.

"Eat something. You need strength for your meeting," he said.

When she smelled the night-blooming flowers waking up outside her window, she decided to take an evening walk. She had cleaned the mud off her sandals and put them on with the black trousers, studded belt, and a new white tank over her palest pink French-lace bra.

Weetzie took the path down to the far end of the hotel, where a row of green-glass shops stood along a reflecting pool in the shade of the palms and jacarandas. She passed a florist; a fancy pharmacy; a bookstore/magazine stand; a gourmet coffee place; a jeweler, a gift shop that sold wind chimes, china fairy and mermaid figurines, paper weights, blown-glass animals, scented candles, and, in an effort to discourage impulsive theft, hotel-room items like bathrobes and satin sheets. There was also Lacey's Beautiful World. The lady from the wedding was standing behind the counter wearing a silk blouse of a fine, loose weave.

"I met you last night!" the lady said. "How are you?"

"Oh, I'm fine. All kinds of strange things are happening. How are you?"

"Everything is beautiful," the woman said. "Isn't it? The air smells so good."

Weetzie nodded, looking through the green glass at the sunset reflected in the long, narrow pool. Purple jacaranda blossoms were drifting down into the water. The lawn was dark velvet-green with shadows.

Weetzie went over to a rack where suits, dresses, and blouses, like the one the woman was wearing, were hanging. They were the softest, most fragile things she had ever felt, but they were strangely strong at the same time, and they glinted with an uncanny light in varying shades of white, cream, gray, and silver.

"Speaking of beautiful!" she said, choosing a silver-white suit with a fitted jacket and short skirt. "Where are these from?"

"I make them," said the woman.

"Are you Lacey?"

She nodded.

"Where do you find the fabric? I've never seen anything like it."

Lacey looked into Weetzie's eyes as if she were trying to figure something out. "You don't seem to me to be the type of person that minds strange things. Am I right?"

"If I was before, I'm not now," said Weetzie. "Everything is strange these days."

"Well then . . ."

Lacey locked the door of the store, sat down, lifted up her shirt so her slim abdomen was exposed. A tiny pair of arms and hands protruded there. Lacey began to move all four hands about with quick, mysterious movements. A milky liquid seemed to be coming out of her, sticking to her fingers in long threads that she wove together. In a short time, she was holding a beautiful, silvery-white scarf. She took a pair of scissors and snipped it off her body.

"How . . ." Weetzie stopped herself. There was no point in asking.

"Just like any woman," Lacey said, handing Weetzie the scarf. "We weave our stories out of our bodies. Some of us through our children, or our art; some do it just by living. It's all the same."

Weetzie took off her clothes and put on the suit. There was no reason to be modest after what she'd just seen. The fabric was so fine that it seemed to melt away at the edges. She bought it on the spot.

"Do you mind me asking, how did you find out you could do this?" she asked.

"Oh, I'm a survivor," Lacey said calmly.

Weetzie waited for her to go on.

"Once, there was this man. I was terrified. I had no idea what I had, what I could do. But all of a sudden, it started happening. I made a web around his face. I got away."

Weetzie wished she knew what to say. Lacey smiled and brushed a piece of hair out of Weetzie's eye.

"You look so great," she said. "Do you have plans?"

"I'm on my own," said Weetzie, and, for the first time since she'd been here, she wished she wasn't.

"Well, have fun! There's a shoe store down the way. Come visit me again."

Weetzie hadn't planned on buying shoes, but she had to go into the little shop when she saw, through the green glass, the twelve dancing girls from the wedding. They were all wearing long gowns and trying on flats. When they saw Weetzie, they rushed out of the door, giggling, and she was left staring at a pair of raspberry snakeskin sandals with precariously high heels and ankle straps.

"Who were those girls?" Weetzie asked the salesman.

"The twelve dancing princesses," he said blithely. "Good customers. They wear everything out in weeks. Those shoes are you!"

Weetzie was so bewildered by the twelve girls that she bought the shoes that instant and wore them out the door. She was almost at the end of the row of shops when she came to a small art gallery. It was closed, but she paused at the window and looked in. A large painting filled the glass. It was of the lower portion of a woman's face—her full mouth and small, sharp chin—and her neck. She had one hand raised, lightly touching her collarbone, where four jewels glimmered as if they were lit from behind the canvas. There was a pearl, a ruby, an emerald, and a sapphire.

Then Weetzie noticed a name written on the glass. ZANE

STARLING. RECENT WORK. The date of the reception was in four days.

Weetzie walked through the gardens to the Japanese restaurant, where she ordered some miso soup, avocado rolls, vegetable tempura, rice, and tofu salad to go. Then she went back to her room, ate, and lay in the dark, in the webby skirt and jacket, wondering what in the world she would say to Zane Starling.

Movies

Weetzie's idea of a business suit was Coco, a white tank top, her new raspberry snakeskin sandals, and her Hello Kitty watch.

She met Dashell Hart and Tristan Sable on the terrace. Tristan, once again, looked very different from his TV self. He wore the thick-rimmed glasses and had his hair in a ponytail. Weetzie tried to see if there was anything bunching up at the back of his T-shirt, but it was too hard to tell. Dashell had on an expensive-looking daffodil-yellow shirt. He smelled like peppermint. Their waiter—Weetzie pretended to be surprised—was Pan.

When she introduced him, Dashell said, "Great name!"

"Yours, too," said Pan. "Both of you."

"You all sound like characters in some crazy book," said Weetzie.

"Oh really?" Dashell peered at her over the top of his

sunglasses. "Weetzie Bat. Talk about overwriting, darling!"

"It's my real name," she said. "I think my dad saw it on a license plate on the freeway in the San Fernando Valley."

"May I suggest the special," Pan said. "Pasta with white beans, garlic, basil, Roma tomatoes, and a touch of olive oil. We can make it without the Parmesan." He winked at Weetzie.

While they were waiting for their pasta, Weetzie asked, "So what's this idea you have?"

Dashell gestured to Tristan, who said, "Well, you know we're big fans of your work. So I thought, maybe do a new piece with your character running away and staying at this hotel. It's just such a great setting. You meet all these weird people and surreal stuff happens, I'm not sure what."

"You meet a charming soap opera angel with actual wings!" said Dashell.

Tristan squirmed. "In the end, you go back to the Max character," he said quickly.

"Is this for Max to direct?" Weetzie asked.

Dashell nodded.

"Because he hasn't worked in a while. He's been sort of down."

"That's the whole point," said Dashell. "A comeback."

"And for you, too," said Tristan.

"You mean I play me?" Weetzie was more excited than she would have expected. She felt color rise in her cheeks.

"Of course, silly." Dashell patted her hand.

"Also," said Weetzie, "I don't mean to be ungrateful, but Max is really into doing things his own way. He's only worked independently before."

"That's what we like," said Tristan. "Right, Dashell?"

"Absolutely. That's the whole point."

Pan came back with the food and left. Weetzie said, "What if my character meets this faun? With furry legs, cloven hooves, and a tail!"

"He does look faunish," said Dashell. "Actually, that might work on the show. What do you think, Tristan?"

Tristan nodded. "I like the faun thing. I don't think it's been done."

They finished their meal with coffee and a tiramisu to share. Weetzie excused herself. Pan met her at the ladies' room door.

"Thank you," he said.

"Do you have your résumé?"

He pulled it out of the back of his pants. "Are you sure this is all right?"

"Of course. They're interested."

"Thank you so much," he said again. His voice quavered a little, which surprised her.

She went back to the table, wishing she had been as excited about helping Max. But maybe this new project would be the thing he needed. Maybe if he looked at her through a camera lens, he would see her again.

When she was saying good-bye to Dashell and Sable, Tristan bent his head and kissed her hand.

Weetzie saw a blond boy sitting in a ditch holding a soiled puppet. It was some kind of soft, furry animal that had once been white but was now quite gray. It had a single sapphire eye.

The boy looked as if he had been beaten—his eyelid was turning pur-

ple and there was blood on his temple and his mouth. His glasses were cracked and broken. He was humming to himself, rocking the lamb back and forth in his arms.

Suddenly, there was a terrible tearing sound. From the young man's bruised, scratched shoulders sprouted huge, white wings.

"Wow!" said Weetzie.

"Does that happen to you a lot?" asked Tristan.

"What?" Dashell asked.

Weetzie turned over her hand and opened her palm, revealing a shockingly bright blue jewel.

"Nice trick, darling," Dashell said. "Can you make me a diamond?"

They got into his Jaguar and disappeared down the hill, through the gate, out of the pink hotel.

Anima/Animus

Weetzie swam laps in the pool that afternoon. Then she had her hair done and got a facial at the cherry-blossom salon. She had to admit that all this talk of movies was making her feel a little self-conscious about her appearance. She couldn't admit to herself that she was getting ready for Zane Starling's art opening.

To distract herself further, she decided to go back to the bar to see Heaven.

Weetzie was sipping her glass of sparkling water, watching the effervescent twinkle of the stars in the ceiling, when a green satin gown descended from a hidden opening in the dome. Inside the dress was Heaven. This time she sang about floating brides, boys with wings, monsters without hearts, and kisses turning to jewels. She sang about how each of us has a male and female self; Weetzie thought of the lady in the lavender sari and what she had said about Zane Starling.

Heaven's last song was about a man who missed his lover so deeply that his soul followed her like a ghost, his footsteps echoing down the path behind her wherever she went.

"Don't cry, girlfriend," she told herself, pretending Ping was here. "You'll ruin your makeup."

After the set was over, a small, wiry young man approached Weetzie's table. He was dressed simply in a black T-shirt, black jeans, and black canvas Converse high-tops. In one ear he wore a single ruby.

"May I join you?" he asked softly.

"Sure," said Weetzie.

"Heaven wanted me to give you this." He handed her a small envelope.

Weetzie found an invitation inside. It read: *Please Come to Heaven's Ball. It's the prom you didn't attend, the wedding you never had, the surprise party no one ever threw for you, the celebration you dream of . . .*

The date of the event was in five nights. Weetzie tucked the invitation into Coco's pocket.

"What did you think of the show?" the man asked.

"It was so beautiful! I don't know how she does it. It's like that song from the seventies, what is it? 'Singing my life with her words.' "

" 'His words.' Roberta Flack, 1973, 'Killing Me Softly.' "

"I'm such a geek, aren't I?" Weetzie said.

"Hey, I'm the one who knows the exact date it came out."

"You would think I was a geek if I told you the first song that made me cry."

" 'Seasons in the Sun.' "

"How did you know?" Weetzie exclaimed. "You're as bad as Heaven."

The man held her eyes with his gaze and smiled wryly.

"Oh," said Weetzie. "Whoops."

"I'm Haven," he said. "Heaven's animus."

Weetzie's skin tingled, as if tiny bubbles were rising up all over under the surface. "Do you think that someone can have their male and female sides so fully developed that they don't need anyone else?" she asked after a while.

He thought for a moment. "Might not need. But when you get what you want it's pretty amazing."

They sat quietly. The stars twinkled in the dome above them.

"I've always been sort of passive," Weetzie said. "I mean, I've done some things, I've had a baby, and raised two babies, plus my boyfriend makes three. I've acted and designed and made clothes and I have a shop and everything, but I don't feel like I've really done anything, you know?"

"That sounds like a lot," said Haven.

"When I was in high school," Weetzie said, "I had this friend, Janet Planet. She was only about five feet tall, really cute, long cartoon eyelashes, dressed in Levi's and checkered Vans. She had this VW Bug and she used to drive around really fast, honking and whistling at cute guys, especially firemen. She was obsessed with firemen. When we all talked about what we wanted to be when we got older, she always said 'a hero.' I thought it was the coolest thing, but it was so different from me."

"What's she doing now?" Haven asked.

"Last I heard she was a firefighter. Until she had her second baby and then she quit."

"Being a good mother is being a hero," said Haven. "Right?"

"My kids are all big now," Weetzie said. "I'm not their hero anymore. I'm not sure I ever was—maybe their storybook princess, when they were really small."

"So what do you want?" asked Haven.

"I want to do something," Weetzie said as a shooting star burned across the glass dome of the bar.

Weetzie and Dirk

Weetzie went to the hotel restaurant for breakfast. While she ate her blueberry pancakes, she glanced up through the glass doors that opened onto the lobby. A tall, dark-haired man in a robin's-egg-blue shirt was standing there.

Weetzie got up and walked straight into his arms.

Smell is a very strange sense, she thought. She remembered hearing once that it is connected to a part of the brain where memory is stored.

He still used the same suntan lotion. They were only eighteen. They surfed all day. Their hair was crusted with salt. Their noses and shoulders were peeling. Dirk pulled his wetsuit off his torso, tied a towel around his waist, and wriggled out of the rest of the suit, then slid on his shorts. He held up Weetzie's towel like a screen for her to change behind. They ate burritos and sat on the sand watching the sun set. They made a campfire and toasted marshmallows. Their fingers were covered with charred, gooey sugar, and their bodies tingled with the heat of the day. Stars came out, and Weetzie and Dirk connected shining dots to find the constellations. The little hairs on their arms touched.

The hair gel once helped a Mohawk defy gravity. They were standing in front of the mirror in the aqua-tiled bathroom. Weetzie shaved the sides of Dirk's scalp with a razor. The skin was so thin at his temples. She thought she could see a pulse there. She held her breath, trying not to imagine his blood.

Dirk's aftershave smelled dry and green, and his breath smelled like good morning coffee under a light coating of peppermint breath mints. Weetzie lay in bed between Dirk and Duck. She was twenty. She was tipsy. When they kissed her, she saw babies swirling around her, little spirits waiting to come.

She didn't realize, until that moment in the pink hotel, how much she had missed Dirk McDonald since she and Max moved out of the house they all shared, back into the cottage.

"You smell like our whole life," Dirk said softly into her hair. "And what else?"

"Blueberry pancakes. Come have breakfast with me."

When they were seated together at the table, he asked her, "When are you coming home, Weetz?"

"Not yet."

"Why? Why are you here?"

She looked around the room. It was flooded with light. The linen napkins were doves ready to fly off. The glasses looked so bright they could have sung. There were crystal vases of orange freesias on each table. The air smelled of butter and maple.

"I'm surprised you're asking me that, of anybody."

"I mean, of course it is beautiful. But I don't get why you did this now."

Weetzie asked, "Why didn't you go to the prom with me?"

"You know that, Weetz."

"Tell me again."

"I wasn't into all the high school hoopdeera."

"And why else?"

"I wasn't ready to tell you I was gay. But at the same time I didn't want you to look back on that night and wonder why your date didn't kiss you. And there was that guy, what was his name?"

"Zane Starling."

"That's right. What kind of name is that, anyway?"

"It's not that strange. Zane is another form of John."

He rolled his eyes. "Where? On Mars?"

"Anyway . . ." she said.

"Anyway, I knew you liked each other. And he was a hot guy. A little odd, but hot. I knew he would ask you and it would be the way it was supposed to be."

"What's that?"

"Hell if I know. Normal. Whatever that is. Kissing. Hot sex. Not having some gay date who can't even admit that to you."

She reached over and squeezed his hand. "I would have loved to go with you, honey."

"What's this all about?" he asked.

"I never even kissed Zane Starling. I was too scared. And I thought, somehow, by coming back here I could understand things better. I'm not sure why. And then, it turns out, he's here—I mean, not here, but he's having an art opening in three days."

"So you want to rekindle this thing with some guy from twenty years ago?"

"No," Weetzie said. "I didn't know he was even going to be here. I just needed to finish something, or figure something out. I don't know what it is. But I can't leave yet."

Dirk nodded. Then he said, "Max is going crazy."

She looked down at the table and moved some bread-crumbs around the linen with her fingernail. "I'm not quite ready," she said.

Dirk reached into his pocket to pay the bill. She touched his hand again. "Will you spend the day with me?"

First he treated her to a massage in her room. They lay next to each other while tall, tan Swedish twins in white rubbed their muscles with scented oils. Then they swam in the pool and lay on the lounge chairs under the green umbrellas. She told Dirk about the kisses and the jewels. None of it seemed to surprise him that much. Since they'd met, their lives were full of magic. Plus, the masseurs alone had convinced him that this wasn't an ordinary place. But he did tell her he was worried when she mentioned Sal, the phone calls for Peri, and the footsteps on the path.

"I'm fine," Weetzie said. "I'm having an adventure."

"I just want you to be safe."

"Dashell Hart wants to make a movie about me, here," she said. "With Max directing."

He glanced around at the tiled pool with its little fountains, at the pink hotel, which looked almost white in the brightness of the day, and the palm trees gleaming gold where the sun touched their fronds. He said, "This would be a great location."

"You should know," said Weetzie. Dirk had a job as a location scout for a major studio. He got paid a lot of money for finding the best mansions and bars and parks and gardens in town, but Weetzie thought he missed working on their little movies.

"And, of course, you'll be perfect," he said.

"I feel a little too old, but it would be fun. I bet we could get you on it, too."

"What about Max?"

"What about him?"

"You'd work with him?"

"Dirk," Weetzie said, "I still love Max. I just had to get away. I have to see."

"What do you have to see? Zane what's-his-name? That waiter guy's curly tail?"

"No," said Weetzie. "It's not that."

"Then what?"

She shrugged and twirled the paper parasol on the cranberry juice and mineral water she had ordered.

"Why did you tell Cherokee and Lily where I was?"

"They were frantic," Dirk said. "They're your kids. What if

your mom did something like this when you were their age?"

Weetzie said, "She did a lot worse." She sipped her drink, imagining a tiny Brandy-Lynn swimming in a martini glass. Was coming to the pink hotel as selfish as that? Would it hurt her girls in the same way?

"But she never went away without telling you where she was. They have a right to know," Dirk said.

"How did you find out, anyway?"

He reached into his pocket and tossed her the hotel matchbox he had picked up after breakfast.

She rolled her eyes. "You've got to stop raiding ladies' purses."

"Listen, Weetz, I was worried about you. And with all this about mutilated mermaids and freaky cell phone messages and stalkers . . ."

"I'm fine," Weetzie said. "I promise."

But that evening, when he was about to go, she hugged him for a little longer than usual, and he looked into her face.

"Do you want me to spend the night?" he asked.

She nodded.

He called Duck to tell him he'd be back in the morning. Then they ordered grilled salmon with cilantro mango chutney from room service.

While they were waiting for the food, Weetzie changed into the suit from Lacey and spun around.

"So she's a spider?"

Weetzie shrugged. "She told me she just started pulling the threads out of her body when that guy attacked her."

"Well, it looks hot on you."

She grinned at him. "You always know how to make a girl feel good." Then, one by one, she took the kissing jewels out of the silk pouch Lacey had given her.

"Wow!" Dirk said. He held the emerald up to the light. "The real thing."

"I think so."

"What are you going to do with them?"

"Heaven said they're for my necklace."

But even as she said that, it didn't feel quite right. Why had she been given the jewels? Did she deserve them? What were they for? What about the family who felt she had abandoned them? Did they need kisses, too? Weetzie closed her eyes and made a wish for Witch Baby and Cherokee, as if the stones were birthday candles or first stars. She wasn't sure what to wish for Max.

Just then the food arrived. It made Weetzie feel calmer right away. The bottle of white wine didn't hurt, either.

"Remember when I used to have to chew pink bubble gum to tolerate the taste of wine?" she giggled.

"Remember when you used to drink champagne with a straw?"

"Remember when I could drink as much rum as you in one sitting?"

"Even though I weigh about twice as much as you."

She put her hands on her stomach. "Oh, God, I don't want to remember drinking that much!"

Dirk said, "But there are so many good things to remember. Duck and I were talking about it the other night—how many amazing things happened for so long and how, now, for the last couple of years, it seems so quiet all the time."

"I think amazing things are happening again," said Weetzie, and she leaned back against Dirk's chest in the big, satiny hotel bed and closed her eyes.

Mermaid

Weetzie woke at dawn. Dirk was sleeping beside her, still wearing all his clothes. She kissed his cheek and went to the pool for a swim. The sky was still gray, just tinged with pink like the perfect shade of powder blush. The air smelled of rain. In spite of the early hour, someone had beaten Weetzie into the water. A woman was moving joyfully under the cool blue mirror that reflected drifting morning clouds. It seemed as if she would never come up for air.

When the woman finally did surface, Weetzie was not surprised to see Shelley. Weetzie was a little taken aback, though, by the fact that the mermaid was completely naked. She tried not to stare at her huge breasts.

"Hi!" Shelley said. It felt like forever before she finally covered her breasts with her robe. "Sal hates me to skinny-dip—isn't that the craziest thing to call it? I mean, some of these things you say. Like, what would a fat-dip be? Wearing lots of sweaters? But anyway, I can't help it sometimes. Luckily, I think he's still asleep."

She glanced up at a window overlooking the pool. Weetzie thought she seemed suddenly anxious.

"How are you?" Weetzie asked.

"Oh, fine, and you?" It sounded rehearsed.

"It's been quite an adventure, being here."

"Really?" Shelley said wistfully. "Not for me, so much. It seems like nothing happens. I eat raw fish and seaweed, go to the salon, collect my mermaids. The best thing is swimming."

"What would you like to be doing?" Weetzie asked.

Shelley glanced up at the window again. Weetzie thought she saw a figure moving behind the drapes.

"I really miss the ocean," Shelley said softly, almost whispering. "And my family. Especially my mother. Sometimes I think I'm going crazy."

Weetzie said, "It must be hard."

"I better go."

"Wait." Weetzie reached out and touched her hand. "I have a car. If you want I can take you someplace."

Shelley's eyes filled with tears but they didn't spill. She wiped them away quickly with the back of the hand Weetzie had touched. "I can't," she said. Her voice was very small, like a child's.

"Are you scared?"

"I have to go."

"I'm in the last garden room by the arbor," Weetzie said. "If you need me."

✳   ✳   ✳

She went to say good-bye to Dirk.

"Please come back soon," he said.

She kissed his cheek. "I will. I think I know what I need to do."

After he left, she spent the rest of the day by the pool. She had brought some hotel stationery and a pen, and on it she made notes to help Tristan Sable with the screenplay for Max.

Mermaid in captivity—plastic surgery mutilation
Faunish waiter
Heaven/Haven explains anima/animus
Changelings
Fairy in Dolce Gabbana
Flying bride w/ munchkins
Spider lady
Soap opera Angel w/ real wings
Jewel kisses
Mysterious footsteps

She stopped at the last note and shivered in the afternoon heat. But she didn't want to think about anything scary.

Finding Zane Starling
What is Max doing now?

This was something she hadn't let herself wonder. It was as if, in order to be here, she had to pretend he was just home alone in the cottage, watching the news and reading the paper. But maybe he was living his own story. She didn't really want to think about this, either.

She ordered a glass of lemonade and some chips and guacamole from the snack bar and kept working. Only once, when she glanced up at Shelley's window, did she think she saw a figure standing there again. And later, just before she headed back to her room to shower and dress for dinner, Weetzie could have sworn she heard a woman sobbing.

How Much
Difference One
Person Can Make

Why are punk shows like ancient pagan rituals?

Witch Baby was sitting in the silent, pale, cathedral-like library, unable to concentrate on the paper she was supposed to be writing. She took the crinkled postcard from Angel Juan out of her pocket. What was it he had been looking for and finally found? Why was he coming back from his trip? Why wasn't he coming here?

Next to the postcard was a flyer Witch Baby had ripped off a kiosk that morning when she was getting her breakfast mushurito. It was for a hardcore punk gig in the city. It might help her with her paper, she told herself. And she needed to get out; she needed a distraction. Sitting here like this was useless.

She got up and walked past the rows of students. Her steel-toed engineer boots echoed on the marble floor. She kept her eyes down, hoping no one was looking at her, wishing she had someone to go with her tonight.

Witch Baby took BART into San Francisco after dark. Then she walked through the Mission to a warehouse where the band was playing. The streets were very dark, mostly deserted. The air felt cool and salty from the bay. Some skinheads walked by, kicking a beer can. One had a large scar down the side of his face. Witch Baby slouched further into her motorcycle jacket—glad she was wearing it, glad she was bald—remembering what Dirk told her before she left for college: shows were more hardcore up north than in L.A.; at least they used to be. She hadn't gone to any yet, but Angel Juan's postcard was like a little animal in her pocket, scratching, nipping; it made her need to keep moving.

Witch Baby sat in the dark warehouse, listening to the ferocious music, watching boys flinging themselves off the stage and slamming into each other in the pit. All boys; there was hardly another girl in the whole place. Witch Baby tried to see something beautiful in the sweaty frenzy of bodies—something ecstatic, like a pagan ritual—but she just felt sad and alone. She imagined ancient rites where nymphs and satyrs played drums and flutes and danced together, celebrating the flow of the wine, the sacred marriage of god and goddess. But there was no sign of the goddess here.

Witch Baby put her hand into the pocket of her leather jacket for Angel Juan's postcard. Instead, she found something else.

Dear Witch Baby,

I know that you stole this jacket from my closet when you left for school. You could have asked me, and of course I would have given it to you! Anyway, I'm glad you have it, because I have a lot of nice memories of wearing it when I was your age. I'm also glad that you and I have similar taste, whether you will admit it or not. But the reason I am writing this is so that when you find it, you will know that I am thinking of you and loving you. I know that you don't like to make yourself vulnerable, but remember, that is the way love comes. Don't be afraid! I love you!

Mom

Witch Baby wondered how she had missed the note all this time. Just then, she looked up and saw a girl sitting by herself, watching her. The girl had short, black hair, a round face, and almond-shaped eyes. She was wearing a fuzzy, brown hooded jacket with ears; it made her look like a bear cub. Witch Baby smiled before she could stop herself, and the girl smiled back. She had a slight overbite. In that dark place, she had the brightest smile Witch Baby had ever seen.

The girl walked over and sat next to Witch Baby. She had to shout to be heard over the music, and her voice made Witch Baby's ears ring. Good pain.

"Hey!"

"Hi," Witch Baby said. She never knew what to say.

"It's too loud over here. Do you want to go get a drink?"

Witch Baby followed her to the bar. They ordered Cokes, and the girl said, "Don't you go to Cal?"

Witch Baby nodded. "I don't think I've seen you."

"I've seen you! I never run into any girls from school at these shows."

Witch Baby looked over at the band. A boy did a somersault off the stage into the crowd. "Why do you come?"

"I don't know. I'm bored. How about you?"

Witch Baby shrugged. She couldn't exactly say that she was lonely. Or could she?

"What's your name?"

"Lily."

"I wish I had a cool name like that. I'm Julie."

"That's a beautiful name."

"You're kidding, right?"

"No. It's great. It's so normal."

"Is that a compliment?"

"Sure. You should hear what my parents call me."

Julie waited. Her eyes were slightly close together, very dark, and a bit sad.

"Witch Baby."

Julie smiled. "Wow! Where'd they get that?"

"They're just crazy," Witch Baby said.

Julie nodded. "Mine are crazy. But in this boring, normal way. At least my dad is. My mom used to be good-crazy."

"What's that?" Witch Baby asked.

"She was an artist in the early eighties—into punk. Actually, I'm named after her best friend, who was this legendary scenester, this beautiful debutante who freaked out her family by moshing at the Mabhuay Gardens but always had this perfect hair and wore the most beautiful vintage dresses with her boots and chains. I actually can't believe my dad let my mom name me after her."

"Why not?" Witch Baby asked.

"He's so conservative. Wants me to be a doctor or some shit. Plus, because of what happened to Julie . . ." She seemed suddenly restless. "Hey, let's get out of here. I know this place that has the biggest burritos you've ever seen!"

They walked down the street to the bright, loud, noisy restaurant, where they gobbled up giant veggie burritos and grilled green onions and sucked on salted slices of lime. Witch Baby thought, It's so strange how much difference one person can make. Not to mention a few letters in a word—the burritos tasted a lot better than the mushuritos she'd been eating.

"Did you take BART?" Julie asked her when they'd finished their food.

Witch Baby nodded.

"Because it is really late and I don't think it's that safe, to be honest. I've got a room in this hotel, if you want to stay."

The hotel was a dark brick building, and Julie's room was tiny and drab, with only one small window that looked out at another dark brick building just a few feet away. But there was something so comforting about being in that room. They lit Nag Champa incense and tiny tea candles that Julie had brought in her backpack, and sat cross-legged on the bed.

"My mom's staying in a hotel right now," Witch Baby said. "Actually, she's not my mom, she's my stepmom. My real mom's basically insane. But, anyway, my stepmother, who is just crazy, is having some kind of midlife crisis or something and she checked into this hotel and she won't tell my dad where she is."

"I love hotels," Julie said. "They are so empty and full at the same time."

Witch Baby nodded. She kind of knew what Julie meant. "I just wish she didn't need to do that now. I mean, why couldn't she have gotten it out of her system when she was young?"

"How old was she when she met your dad?"

"Like, nineteen or something."

Julie shrugged. "She didn't have a chance, I guess."

"What about your mom?" asked Witch Baby. "Would she do that?"

"No, but she should."

"I'm just so afraid of turning into my stepmom," Witch Baby said. "I mean, she's cool and everything, but she never really had a life of her own. She's always been there for everybody else."

"I hear that," said Julie.

"I have this boyfriend," said Witch Baby. "We've known each other since we were little kids. He's been all over the world and now he's coming back to L.A. and I think he wants to be with me. But I haven't really done anything yet. I mean, even being in Berkeley is like a big deal or something."

Julie nodded. Witch Baby felt herself getting drowsy. Her eyes closed.

A Chinese girl with long, black hair and a blond girl wearing a pale blue lace dress were sitting in a large, dark ornate nightclub, holding bouquets of fake red-silk roses. Boys and girls with Mohawks, tattoos, and pierced faces were swarming around them. One of the boys leaned down and bit the blonde on the neck.

Witch Baby's eyes popped open.

"What ever happened to Julie?" she asked.

"You mean my mom's friend? She died of AIDS," Julie said. "She was only twenty."

Witch Baby shivered.

"If she hadn't died, my mom would have been an entirely different person," Julie said. "But then, I might not be here, either."

Witch Baby said softly, "Isn't it weird how much difference one person can make?"

Cherokee
and the Sphinx

Cherokee and Raphael woke at the same time and lay holding each other, watching the rainbows on the wall from the sun kissing the old flea-market chandelier crystals they had hung in the window. Cherokee had cramps from her period, so Raphael rubbed her belly gently. After so many years together, they knew exactly what each other's bodies needed.

"There's going to be a good swell this morning," Raphael said.

Cherokee groaned. "I've got a bad swell inside me. I think I'll just watch today."

While he surfed, she sat on the sand, wrapped in a heavy Mexican blanket. The sea breeze whipped stray hairs across her face; her fingers absently popped open juicy pods on the thick strands of seaweed she was weaving together. She could see Raphael cresting a wave—his body crouched, poised, part of the ocean. Usually they went into the water together. She loved surfing with him. And she loved music and dancing and clothes. But what did she really want? What did she love enough to spend her whole life doing? At least Weetzie had her own shop, and she'd made those movies. What if Cherokee got old like that and still hadn't done anything? Maybe she wouldn't run away to a hotel to find love she had lost; maybe she would run away to find something she loved to do.

Raphael ran up the beach in his wet suit and dripped salt water from his dreadlocks onto her upturned face. She could see the form of his body perfectly silhouetted against the dazzling morning horizon. She wanted, somehow, to create something even partly that beautiful.

"How was the water?" she asked as he dropped down on his knees beside her.

"Good. I missed you, though. And I'm starved."

They went to their favorite greasy spoon on State Street and sat in the back patio with the ceramic sun ornaments and the peeling maritime mural, eating huevos rancheros. Cherokee was quieter than usual. She knew she should be happy to be here with him, having their favorite meal, but she just didn't feel it. Maybe because of her period.

"What's wrong, Kee?"

"I've been thinking about Weetzie," she said.

"That hotel thing really got to you, ay?"

"I was just thinking, what if I spend my whole life having fun, hanging out, not sure what I really want to do? Then I turn forty and I realize I haven't really done anything. She's running away but at least she's done some cool stuff."

"You're still young, babe. You'll figure it out. And, besides, you've done some amazing things already. Just the way you can make things is incredible."

"I haven't made anything for years," Cherokee said.

Neither mentioned the wings, but they were both thinking about them. Years ago, Cherokee had constructed a pair of wings for her sister, Witch Baby. They were huge, intricate, covered with a rainbow of feathers. They had helped lift Witch Baby out of her sorrow. And then things turned strange. The wings had too much power. After they flew off by themselves, Cherokee vowed never to create anything like them again.

"I don't even know what my major is," Cherokee said, trying somehow to make things feel normal. "I feel like I'm here to be with you and that's about it."

He rubbed her bare knee. "I'm a lucky man."

She kissed him and smiled, but the sadness still lay inside of her, curled up like a sleeping animal, ready to awaken.

When they got back to the apartment, there was a large box waiting on the doorstep. They brought it inside and Cherokee tore it open.

"It's the Sphinx!" she said.

"What?"

"The Sphinx sewing machine. It's an early-model Singer. I can't believe she sent this. She must have done it before she went away."

Attached to the sewing machine was a little note.

✳   ✳   ✳

Cherokee,

Once, when you were younger, you made a pair of wings for your sister. I know that some scary things happened after that. But I want to tell you, I think you have grown into your magic now. Use it well.

Love,
Mom

Suddenly Cherokee felt badly about how she had treated Weetzie at the pink hotel. Especially what she had said about her clothes. Weetzie was right—that was just mean-spirited. Her mother had been her fashion idol since Cherokee could remember. Not that Cherokee planned on ever letting her know that she still felt this way, of course.

Raphael showered for class, and Cherokee sat at the black-and-gold sewing machine, rubbing her hands along its smooth sides. She knew that it had once belonged to Dirk's Grandma Fifi, and there was a long story about it before that, but she never really paid attention to those things. Now she wished she had; the machine seemed to hold a secret, like a real Sphinx.

Cherokee did not go to class that day. Instead, she stayed home and made sketches of the pictures she had seen in her mind for years, and been afraid to see. She sketched sleek, stretchy, wet suit–inspired outfits with zippers everywhere, which unzipped into smaller and smaller pieces of clothing. She made sketches of tiny minidresses under buoyant wire-hoop skirts overlaid with tulle. She sketched iridescent shark-skin suits, sweaters and knit pants trimmed with pale feathers, sheer voile trench coats over narrow trousers and tank tops, and slim dresses, coats, and hats made of hundreds of dew-drop beaded silk taffeta petals. She drew clear, heart-shaped charms filled with dried flowers, stars, tiny dolls, bits of po-etry, and pictures of goddesses, to use on the pulls of zippers. She imagined that each piece of clothing would have little se-cret spells written into the lining—incantations that would make the wearer feel her beauty and her power.

That was what clothing could do, Cherokee realized. It could seduce, soothe, enhance, disguise, protect. It could em-power. Like magic. And Weetzie had said Cherokee had grown into her magic now.

Then Cherokee thought about her mother making her own kind of magic at the pink hotel. Transforming her own life, and maybe theirs. Cherokee was suddenly no longer afraid.

Amethyst Kiss

Weetzie had eaten a bento box of soba noodles, rice, sautéed tofu, seaweed, and pickled vegetables at the Japanese restaurant and was walking through a bamboo grove back to her room. Santa Anas played the stalks like an instrument.

She paused by a small stone pagoda and looked up at the moon. Was Max looking at it, too, this instant? It seemed strange to her that he hadn't tried to call her all this time. Maybe the girls hadn't told him where she was, but he could at least have tried her cell phone. She shivered, remembering the voice messages she had received. At least the messages had stopped since Peri and Bean left, and so had the footsteps. She hoped her friends were all right and had reached their destination. Maybe the warlock would protect them. Maybe the elf king would find them.

This hotel has done some strange things to me, Weetzie thought. Mostly, it has made nothing seem strange anymore.

The memory of the obscene-sounding voice on her phone was still shivering up and down her spine, so when she heard someone behind her, she whirled around right away, brandishing her hotel key.

"It's me," Pan said. "Careful with that thing."

Embarrassed, she dropped the key back into her purse. "Sorry, I'm a little on edge."

"Why is that?"

She didn't want to say it was because she hadn't made love in almost two years, she had received phone messages about abusing one's private parts, that since she'd come here she was sure she was being followed, that there had been three nightmarish people with an empty baby carriage on the path, and that she believed Sal had captured and mutilated a mermaid.

"Thank you for your help," Pan said as they walked. "Dashell Hart called me today. I have an audition next week."

"That's wonderful!" said Weetzie.

"I know it sounds kind of stupid, but it means a lot to me. I've wanted this chance forever. It gets frustrating."

Weetzie stopped and smiled up at him. "I'm so glad."

There was a heavy silence. Weetzie looked up at the sky. "What a pretty night! Look at that moon!"

"And you're a moon girl," said Pan.

She was wearing her white satin trench and her white jeans; her freshly bleached hair shimmered.

She moved away from him.

"Well, I just wanted to thank you. I'll let you go."

He started to leave, but Weetzie grabbed his large, smooth wrist. It felt like marble, except for the heat and pulse. "Wait. Will you do me one favor?"

He grinned, flashing the gap between his teeth.

"Can I kiss you?"

A TV screen was buzzing with static that then dissolved to let Weetzie tumble through into a kitchen. A woman who looked like a depressed Italian movie star was watching a soap opera and drinking red wine. A little boy with curly hair tugged on her skirt, but she shooed him away as the actors kissed. The boy tried to take her hand, on which gleamed a ring with a purple stone, but she pulled it away. He gazed at her wistfully and then went outside, into an overgrown garden. As he ran through the flowerbeds, the garden changed, becoming more and more wild until it was a forest. The boy stripped off all his clothes and kept running. He splashed through shallow streams, rolled in piles of leaves, plastered mud all over his body. Weetzie could see him from the back as he ran deeper into the trees.

He had a small, erect tail protruding at the base of his spine. Suddenly he turned around and held something up.

It was a many-faceted purple jewel.

Weetzie spit the amethyst out into her hand. Before she could show it to him, Pan was gone.

This time she thought at first that she must have imagined the footsteps. After all, even Pan had made her jump just a short time earlier. She was sure Peri's monstrous family was gone. Who would want to bother her here? But then she thought of the shadow in the room above the pool and wondered if Sal might have a reason to hate her. If he didn't yet, she thought he might soon. She glanced behind her. The path was empty. Even so, Weetzie ran the rest of the way back to her room and locked the door.

Hilda

Hilda Doolittle was sitting behind the counter in the sunny front room of Weetzie's, eating a Krispy Kreme doughnut and writing poetry in her journal, when her boyfriend, Ezra, walked in. She thought of hiding the doughnut but it was too late. She put it down and wiped the sugar off her fingers, though she wanted to lick them, and quickly closed her journal.

"What's up, Hilda?" Ezra said. He started walking around, running his fingers over the beaded dresses. With the click of each bead, Hilda winced. She hoped Ping wouldn't come back now.

"Not much."

"Is this your poetry?" he asked.

She put her sticky hands on the journal.

"I was thinking," he said. "How serious are you about this poetry stuff?"

"You know the answer to that, Ezra."

"Well then." He walked over to her and leaned on the counter. She could feel his warm breath. The goatee he had grown recently made him look like the devil. His eyes were cold and sparkling. She had no idea why she loved him so much. "I've been wanting to tell you a few ideas I have."

She waited. Her fingers still felt gluey with sugar. She wished that she had worn the pink-and-black lace dress with the sweetheart neckline and borrowed the pink rhinestone chandelier earrings from the jewelry case. Instead, she had on a black beaded sweater that made her sweat, and an itchy black skirt.

"First," he said, leaning closer, "we need to do something about those glasses."

He reached up, very carefully, and removed her frames, without touching any part of her. Panic drummed at her throat. She wanted to snatch back her glasses but instead she smiled at his blurry face.

"And, Hilda," said Ezra, "remember what we talked about—no more sugar."

She heard the soft, crumpling sound of the greasy dough-nut bag as he took it. She heard him rummage around, find a Krispy Kreme, and take a bite.

"I don't mean to be harsh but it's a tough world out there," Ezra said, his mouth full of doughnut. "You've really got to look like a rock star to read at a coffee house in L.A. these days."

Hilda kept smiling but she felt sick. Her hands went to her thighs. The black skirt was too tight. Why had she worn it?

Ezra said, "There's another thing. I'm not thrilled with your name. I keep thinking you should try to find something catchier. Maybe something with a little hip-hop vibe. Hot Dawg." He laughed. "Just kidding. How about Big H?"

She thought he was raising his hand in a high five, so she held hers up shyly, but he didn't slap her palm, so she pretended she was fixing her hair.

"I have more ideas, too, but I have to go now."

Hilda heard him toss her glasses back on the counter. "My brother had that laser surgery on his eyeballs," Ezra said. "He's got twenty-twenty now. They burn the cornea or something; it's really cool. Later."

He was gone. Hilda put on her glasses and picked up her poetry book. She didn't even know why she wanted to cry.

Don't I Know You?

What do you wear to an art opening of work by a man whom you should have kissed over two decades ago?

In the morning, Weetzie went to the hotel jewelers, carrying the pouch that Lacey had given her. Inside it was a pearl, a ruby, an emerald, a sapphire, and an amethyst.

"Is it possible to have these set by tonight?" she asked the diminutive man behind the counter.

He squinted up at her with his pale eyes. He was wearing a silk turban and had a long, grizzled beard. His hands were fine and as quick as little brown birds. Jewels twinkled, starlike, on midnight-blue velvet in the glass case. Hot-pink, electric-blue, and gold sari fabric covered the cushions on the ornately carpeted floor.

"Don't I know you?" he said.

Weetzie, who did not think that anything could surprise her anymore, gasped.

"You're him!" she said.

"What brings you here?"

"I'm escaping."

"Escaping? How ungrateful. I appear to you, out of a lamp, of all things, and grant you three wishes, any three wishes, and now you're escaping?"

"What are *you* doing here?"

"This happens to be my hotel! I like to pop in every now and then to see how things are going."

Weetzie sat down on a stool in front of the counter and rubbed her eyes. When she opened them, the man was still there. He twirled his whiskers, rather madly.

"Did I wish for the wrong things?" She tightened her fingers around the silk pouch of jewels.

"Who is to say? You wished for your heart's desire. Now it has changed."

"But it hasn't," Weetzie said.

"Then why did you come here?"

"I wished for a duck man for Dirk, and he came. They're still in love, like the day they met. I wished for a little house to live in, and Dirk's Grandma Fifi died and left us her cottage and I still live there. I wished for my secret agent lover man," she said. "But now he isn't. Maybe he never was."

"Why do you say that? Because he watches the television all the time? Because he is sad? Because his heart is broken?"

"I tried to wish for world peace," Weetzie said. She felt her throat close up. "You said it wouldn't work."

"I'm afraid not. Alas. Your world leaders keep getting stupider and stupider."

"Then what do we do?"

"Make your own peace?" the man said. "Now, pearls for transformation, rubies for passion, emeralds for fertility, sapphires for truth, amethyst against intoxication. Let me see what I can do with those jewels of yours."

Zane Starling

So, that evening, Weetzie wore the necklace made of gifts from a mermaid, a diva, a fairy, an angel, and a faun, and fashioned by a genie who, years before, Weetzie had set free from his lamp. With it, she wore her pink sandals and a strapless white satin minidress she had made with a sheet from the gift store, using her miniature hotel sewing kit.

She arrived at the gallery a little late, because it had taken her longer than she thought to finish making the dress. People were spilling out of the door and sipping champagne in plastic cups around the reflecting pool. Weetzie shouldered through the crowd to look at the painting in the front window. She noticed that something had changed, but she wasn't sure what.

A waiter came by with a glass of champagne and she took it, wondering if Pan's amethyst would keep her from becoming too drunk. It didn't seem to work; soon she was on her fourth glass. The bubbles stung her nose, and her knees wobbled. She felt full of golden light. Another waiter came by with a tray of hors d'oeuvres and she was suddenly so hungry; she had been too excited and too busy sewing to eat. Then another waiter with a tray, and another. She devoured potato puffs, crab cakes, mini quiches, shrimp satay. She washed it all down with more champagne and stumbled around, looking at the art.

Zane Starling's paintings were huge and disarmingly lifelike in spite of their subject matter. There was a painting of a woman with a mermaid's tail holding the hand of her bleeding, two-legged twin. There was naked hermaphrodite with rubies coming out of his/her mouth. There was a red-haired pregnant woman with a whip riding on the back of a man with pointed ears. There was a faun with hairy haunches, a tail, cloven hooves, and devilish horns, masturbating, watching a large TV with a handsome, blond angel on the screen. The angel had a baby lamb in his arms.

Weetzie went back to the painting in the front window. She looked at it carefully and realized that there was a new jewel on the woman's necklace—an amethyst, just like the one from Pan. It must have been the champagne, but she could have sworn she saw the woman's lips curl into an eerie smile.

Then she turned around.

A tall man standing in a crowd of people.

He was wearing a white T-shirt, blue jeans, and heavy-soled black shoes. His straight blond hair was graying at the temples and cut very short. Except for the gray and a slight crepeyness around his smiling eyes, Zane Starling looked just the same as he had looked over twenty years ago.

Weetzie touched her throat where the necklace felt cool against her pulse. She smoothed her hands over her dress, suddenly embarrassed to be wearing a sheet. Then she walked over to him.

"Excuse me? May I talk to you for a minute?"

He nodded politely to the people around him and walked with her over to the front of the gallery. She gulped at the cool night air that came through the door. Sweat trickled down the sides of her neck.

"How are you?"

"Oh, fine. How are you tonight?" he said. His voice was kind, but his eyes were darting back and forth over her face; she wasn't sure that he knew who she was, but she couldn't bring herself to tell him yet. Maybe he would remember.

"I saw the painting in the window. I'm staying here, in the hotel, and I couldn't believe it! It was such a weird coincidence. I've been wanting to see you. I wanted to tell you something."

He smiled, but this time he looked a little wary.

"I'm Weetzie," she said. "Weetzie Bat? We went to the prom together."

"Of course. Weetzie." The skin around his green eyes crumpled softly. "You look just the same. I just couldn't place you."

"Can we go outside for a second?" she said. She was feeling as if she might faint. The naked hermaphrodite on the wall winked at her, but it might have been the champagne.

The moon was mirrored in the reflecting pool, a huge, floating lotus. The little glass shops along the water were all closed. Weetzie glanced over at the jewelers, but it was completely dark inside.

"Your work is so beautiful!" Weetzie said. "It's so magical, and I try not to use that word too much because it is so sacred to me, you know? I like this word 'numinous,' because it's not overused—it's not even in every dictionary—and it sounds like luminous, which is another word I love and it means 'supernatural, mysterious, a sense of the presence of divinity.' I always thought that if anyone ever asked me to be on that program *Inside the Actors Studio*—not that they would ask me—I don't know if you've seen any of the movies I've been in—*Dangerous Angels* is one—not that James Lipton, the host guy, would ask me to be on, but you know, it's a fantasy—that I would say 'numinous' when they asked me what my favorite word was. And I guess 'pustule' is my least favorite word, or maybe 'pitiful.'"

She stopped. "Oh, God, I sound so pitiful. What am I talking about?"

"It's all right," he said. She wished he wasn't so nice. She wished there was something imperfect about him.

"Anyway, what I wanted to say was, I'm so sorry I pushed you away that night. On our prom. You were too much for me, I think. This lady I met at a wedding, she said you are my animus but I wasn't ready for you yet. I was too young. I didn't like myself enough or something. Anyway, I just wanted to say I'm sorry."

He nodded patiently, but she could tell he wasn't really

following her. It struck her that if he had been upset at all about what had happened, he had forgotten it a long time ago.

"That's very nice of you, but don't worry about it," he said. He smiled over her head at someone. "I'm glad you could come to the show."

"I meant to ask you," Weetzie said quickly, "who is that a painting of?" She pointed to the woman in the window. She hadn't let herself even think it before, but the picture did resemble her, not to mention her necklace of kisses.

"Oh, that's my wife, Karen. I wish you could meet her but she's at home with the kids. And she has her practice. She's a therapist."

"How many kids do you have?" Weetzie asked.

Zane Starling pointed over to another painting. It showed a woman with six arms. In the palm of each hand she held a tiny baby. In her belly was a self-portrait of Zane Starling, sleeping peacefully. The woman had pale skin, rosy cheeks, long, brown hair, and blue eyes. Weetzie was not sure if it made her feel relieved or sad that she did not resemble Tracy Calla. Except for something about her chin, mouth, and neck, she looked nothing like Weetzie, either.

"Six. The oldest is in college and the baby is five. Every time Karen gave birth she'd say what a miracle it was and shouldn't we see what other combination we could come up with, so . . . but I have to keep selling a lot of work."

"Where are you living?" asked Weetzie.

"We have a house in Upstate New York. You should visit sometime."

"Thank you," said Weetzie, but it wasn't for the invitation.

He had not blinded her. He had not kissed her. He had freed her.

Weetzie felt something scratchy in her eye. She rubbed it with the back of her hand. A tiny spark of a jewel slid down her cheek encased in a tear. It was recognizable as a diamond, even to a rhinestone fanatic. Weetzie handed it to Zane Starling. Then she left.

Coyote

Max rode his motorcycle out to Joshua Tree to visit his friend Coyote. Coyote lived in a sand-colored adobe house near the monument and held sweats in the lodge he had built. He rode his horse, Luna, through the Joshua trees at sundown. He watched the sky, followed the cycles of the moon. He never missed Los Angeles; Coyote wondered why he had ever lived there at all.

Max rode under the arching gray bridges of freeway, past minimalls, gas stations, greasy fast-food places, casinos, strips of empty highway and dry brush with billboards for topless bars and retirement living. The air smelled foul; his eyes stung. He stopped at a rest area to use the men's room and kept thinking about how people disappeared at places like this. He wondered if he might disappear, now that Weetzie was gone.

Finally he got to the windmills on the hill. The air began

to feel cleaner. There was a powdered-sugar sprinkle of snow on the distant mountains. The horizon danced with blue heat.

Max rode through the desert cities. He imagined finding a little cabin and living out here with the roadrunners and the bats. Each town had a market, a bank, a gas station, a video store, a used bookstore, cheap Chinese food, coffee, cigarettes, beer. What else could anyone want? Max thought to himself. Right? I'll collect scraps of metal and other junk to put in my yard, among the cactus plants and creosote. I'll sit on my dilapidated porch and drink my coffee and smoke some weed and try to learn what the stars are saying. In a place this dry and colorless, I will not be able to think of her.

When he arrived at Coyote's, they did sit on the porch and drink coffee and Max smoked a little pot he'd brought, but, of course, he did not stop thinking of Weetzie for a moment.

"I wish I were more like you," he said to his friend.

"And why is that?"

"You are so centered all the time. Like you don't need anyone in order to be okay."

Coyote tossed his head and laughed, bitter and deep as the coffee they were sipping. "Let me tell you something. The other day this guy came to one of my sweats—Native American dude, very angry, very hard. He started laying into me at one point about everything—my name, the way I spoke. He goes, 'You think you are the noble savage? It's every fucking cliché there is, man. Get off this high horse, you are so full of shit,' things like that. I didn't say anything; I just walked away. He was wrong and he was right. Have I ever told you about who I really am?"

Max shook his head, a little ashamed. Should he have asked? Listened better? They had known each other since they were twenty. Coyote had always been someone he admired so much. Maybe he didn't want to look past the grace.

"See, my dad, he *was* that guy—drunk, womanizer, pissed off. He beat the shit out of us. I was becoming him at sixteen, but I didn't want it. So I changed my name and left my family and tried to be perfect." He laughed again but his eyes flickered darkly. "And now this asshole comes into my lodge and tells me I am a cliché. Because I try to be pure. Because I try to be what we once were."

"But you do it," said Max.

Coyote shook his head. "You don't really know me," he said.

Max looked out over the desert. A light rain was beginning to fall, coaxing fragrance out of the earth, the sweet-acrid-green smell of creosote rising up. The bright moon made the raindrops glisten and cast strange, twisted shadows of Joshua trees. Lily, his witch baby, had once told him that those plants, which only grew in a few places in the world, were actually a type of flower. She had said, "A weird lily, like me." He realized with regret that he hadn't disputed this—that she had called herself weird; he was too busy thinking it wasn't a surprise she was a little odd—his child and Vixanne's. It was incredible that she had turned out as healthy as she had. Probably because Weetzie had raised her.

"She left me."

"I figured that was why you came."

"I dream of her all the time. In the dreams I am following her down this path. She hears my footsteps behind her and she is afraid but she can't see me."

Coyote nodded and took a drag on Max's joint. His face was lined. His hair was pulled back in a long braid. He wore a tattered Western shirt, Levi's, and boots. Max remembered seeing Coyote sprinting through the streets of Hollywood, wearing a fringed suede jacket, with his long, black hair streaming behind him. He was so young. Max had driven by and honked and waved. Coyote waved back, laughed, and kept running. Max realized that his friend had never seemed real before. He had been like a symbol of something wise and beautiful and perfect that Max could never attain, but that could guide him.

He could still guide him. Maybe better than ever.

"Let's sweat," Coyote said.

Before they entered the lodge, they knelt on the ground in the rain and dug up clumps of mud with their hands.

Coyote said, "Make your spirit," and Max found the clay becoming a large dog that resembled a horse, though he had planned on making some kind of mutt.

The lodge smelled of cedar and eucalyptus. Sweat poured out of Max until he couldn't see anymore. He felt every pore of his body opening.

"I can't stop seeing the people jumping," Max said.

Coyote nodded.

"What do you do with that kind of pain?"

Coyote pointed to the clay dog in Max's hand. "Give it to

him to carry. The strong part of yourself." Then he said, "Once, I went to see a very wise man. I saw him once a week for months. Every time I went there I sat and talked about how fucked up the world was. I was getting more and more frantic. Poverty, disease, war. He listened and listened. Finally he said, 'What happened to you when you were a boy?' And I said, 'My father beat me every day.' "

Max smoothed his thumb over the clay dog. He did not look at his friend.

"Maybe it is time to look at the disasters inside of you," Coyote said gently. He began to hum, deep in his throat.

Max closed his eyes. He saw a little boy sitting in a dark closet. Someone was pounding on the door of the boy's room so that the walls shook.

Sweat, or maybe tears, poured down Max's cheeks. It was only the beginning of remembering.

Later, as they lay on their backs on Coyote's adobe roof, looking at the constellations, Max asked, "Why death, do you think?"

"The Iroquois say that the world was too full, so the men and women got together, separately, to find an answer. The men came up with the idea of not having any more children. But the women refused to give up having babies. Death was their answer."

Max nodded. He took a deep breath. It felt like he hadn't breathed like that in months, maybe years.

Coyote said, "She needed a pink hotel. What about you? What's your pink hotel?"

Max didn't have to think about it. "She is," he said.

Ghost

Maybe she was too drunk to notice, but no one followed her home that night. She took off her pink sandals and lay down on her bed. The room spun, not unpleasantly, like riding a carousel. Her fingers touched the stones in the necklace of kisses. One by one. The pearl looked like a little moon. The ruby reminded Weetzie of shining blood, and the emerald was leaves in the sun. The sapphire was a burning lake. The amethyst, flowers on fire. But each jewel was so much more than these things, too.

Shelley. Heaven. Peri. Tristan. Pan. Her eyelids closed.

There was a soft rapping sound at the French doors. But there was no wind tonight. More curious than afraid, though she didn't know why, Weetzie jumped up and hid behind the curtains. Then she peeked out into the garden. A faint milky light was hovering over the plants—a dream of sleepy flowers.

As soon as she saw it, Weetzie wanted the light to come into her room.

"It's me," a voice said.

She opened the doors and the light poured in. It hovered above the carpet, illuminating the flowers on the wallpaper, making them seem alive. Then the light began to take form, like a TV image swarming with static before it comes into focus—head, body, arms, legs, feet—the figure of a man.

"I hope I didn't give you the utzies."

But she wasn't uneasy at all. She had been waiting.

"Daddy?" said Weetzie. "Why did it take you so long?"

"I can't say that was the response I expected," he said. His voice was the same—gravelly, cracking from cigarettes and booze—just fainter. "I thought you'd think you were dreaming."

"Not anymore," said Weetzie. "It's all a dream."

"I didn't come because you didn't call for me."

"I didn't think you'd hear me."

He shrugged. His limbs were long and loose, like a marionette's, in his dark suit. He had shadows beneath his eyes and in the hollows of his cheeks. Weetzie had imagined this so many times, for so many years. How he would return to her. How he would put his arms around her. She would feel his scratchy chin and smell the smoke in his jacket. But now she had no desire for him to hold her. Her hand went numb and she flexed her fingers to bring the heat and circulation back.

"I didn't call tonight," she said. "Did I?"

"No. Someone else."

Weetzie looked at her father's ghost. She thought she saw a blurry X-ray of bones and organs beneath his clothes. Where the heart should have been was only light. She twisted the ring on her finger.

"Max," she said.

"He's been following you," said Charlie Bat.

Weetzie's other hand went numb. She was remembering the sound of footsteps on the path. Had Max been there? Had he been watching her this whole time? Had he seen her kiss anyone?

"Not his body. He can't help it. He dreams of you and a part of his spirit follows you. He doesn't mean to scare you, baby. He doesn't know it, but tonight he sent me instead."

She imagined Max lying in their bed at home, dressed in his coat and trousers, curled up on his side. She could see his organs and bones through his clothes. His heart was still there—still beating—but he was turning into a ghost.

"Why?" she asked.

"He wants you to come home, Weetzie."

"Daddy?" she said. "Why did you leave?"

He had left her twice, once when he fought with Brandy-Lynn and drove away in the yellow Thunderbird, his clothes soaked with the gin she had thrown at him, once with a handful of pills in a dark corner in his apartment in New York City. All she had wanted, both times, was for him to come back and hold her, as if that would take all the sadness away. But when he died it was Max who put his arms around her and tried to take her sadness into him, along with all his own sadness, the unfathomable sadness of the world.

Charlie did not answer. He had left a third time. The room was dark, the garden beyond the French doors was dark, and there was a chill in the room.

Morning

The breakfast she had ordered the night before was sitting on her doorstep—fruit salad, a poached egg, and fresh-squeezed orange juice. On the tray there was also a small china mermaid figurine with big, surprised-looking eyes and long, green hair. Weetzie turned it upside down right away. There was a piece of paper tucked into the opening at the base of the figure. It read: *help midnite xxx pamela.*

She ate, bathed, and dressed in her white tank over an orange French-lace bra, her orange zippered pants, and her orange sneakers. She was still wearing the jeweled necklace from the night before.

Weetzie sat down at the yellow desk and added some notes to the list for Tristan Sable:

The genie returns
Meeting Zane Starling

A diamond tear
The ghost in the garden
Be a hero!
Then what?

At the end of the list she wrote, "Call me and we'll talk about these some more! Weetzie."

She put the notes into an envelope, addressed it to Dashell Hart, who had slipped her his card at their last lunch, got a postage stamp at the front desk, and mailed the notes to Dashell and Tristan. Then she walked to the row of shops. They were all open except for the jewelers; inside, it was completely dark. But Weetzie knew she didn't need the genie anymore. Instead, she went to see Lacey at her Beautiful World.

"I need your help," she said. "How strong is your web? Can it catch very, very big flies?"

"How big? How nasty?"

"Big and nasty," Weetzie said.

Lacey smiled.

Next, Weetzie went to the Cherub suite. She wasn't sure who answered the door. The person was wearing an electric-blue kimono and headscarf—and needed a shave. Weetzie checked the feet to see if they would give her a clue. They were bare, with clear-polished toenails.

"I'm sorry to disturb you so early," Weetzie said.

"It's all right," said Heaven. "Come in, sweetheart."

Weetzie went inside and sat down with Heaven on a settee with gold wings. Heaven handed Weetzie a small envelope.

"What can I do you for?"

"This may sound very silly," said Weetzie.

"Silly? I love silly! Where would we be without it?"

"I just wondered if—this may be presumptuous—but I wondered if there was anything I could help you with."

Heaven grinned, coyly placed a hand between her own legs, and said, "That kiss wasn't too bad. I could use a nice rock."

Weetzie's eyes widened.

"You know, a ruby earring! No, just kidding. I only kiss when I really know the person. Or if it's a game of spin the bottle!"

Weetzie said, "Because I realized that I've spent this whole time here indulging myself and I'd like to do something that matters a little. So if there's anything you'd like . . ."

Heaven reached out and touched Weetzie's hand. She touched Max's gold ring.

"Are you leaving us?"

Weetzie nodded. "Soon."

"Did you get what you came for?"

"Almost," Weetzie said. "There's something else I have to do first."

"Come to my ball, tomorrow night," said Heaven. "But besides that, what did you think you could do for me?"

"I have no idea, really. I told you it was silly. I just wanted to try."

"Because you already have done something for me,

sweetie," Heaven said. "Congratulations. It only took you—what—about four decades, but still!"

"What?" Weetzie asked.

And Heaven said, "Why, Weetzie Bat, you've grown up, of course."

The Goddess

On the way back from the desert, Max stopped at Weetzie's store. He wasn't sure why he was doing this; he knew she wasn't there and he wouldn't know what to say to Ping if she was working. But he just wanted to be inside.

The salesgirl, Hilda, was talking to a guy with a goatee. Max walked around the shop. Everything was carefully and sparsely arranged on gleaming racks. There were forties satin slips; fifties party dresses and beaded sweaters; sixties minis; seventies bell-bottoms and print blouses. There were denim jackets and jeans appliquéd with silk flowers, wool coats embellished with jewels, and handpainted tuxedos. The wood floor, white walls, windows, and mirrors sparkled. The air did not smell of old clothing, only of Woolite and roses.

Max chose a black tuxedo with a white rose painted on the lapel, a pair of gold pointy-toed pumps with very high heels, and elbow-length pink gloves. He went up to the counter and waited for Hilda.

The goatee guy left, and Hilda turned around, not aware that Max was there. She had tears in her eyes, magnified behind her large, black-framed glasses.

"Hilda?" said Max. "You okay?"

She tried to smile and dabbed at her eyes with an embroidered cotton handkerchief. "Oh, yeah. Sorry. Are you going to take that stuff?"

"And I'd like to buy the dress up there."

Max pointed above the counter to a frothy white gown. It had a strapless, pleated satin bodice and a huge tulle skirt made of silk roses.

"Princess Grace?" Hilda said.

"Is that what she calls it?"

"Her. That's Weetzie's Princess. I'll put it all in the book."

"I'm buying it. Her."

"Don't you want to just take her?"

"No," said Max. "I'm paying. No discount, either."

"Okay." Hilda went to ring him up. "How's Weetzie?" she asked. "I haven't seen her for a while."

Max said, "She's taking a little time for herself."

"Oh," said Hilda. She looked at him more closely. "Are you okay?"

Max said, "Do you want the truth or the polite answer?"

"The truth," said Hilda. "Always the truth."

"Not okay."

"Me either."

"Do you want to talk about it?"

She looked down at the cash register. "That guy who was here, that's Ezra."

"Ezra?"

"Yeah. He's my boyfriend, I think. Anyway, he's always on me about something. Like he wants me to lose weight and get rid of my glasses. He even wants me to change my name. He thinks Hilda Doolittle is a bad name for a poet. What do you think?"

Max said, "There was a poet in the twenties named Hilda Doolittle. You don't know her?"

Hilda shook her head.

"She wrote this spare, beautiful stuff and she saw a goddess in Greece."

Hilda's eyes widened, behind her glasses.

"And *Ezra* Pound changed her name to H.D."

"H.D. That's cool. Who is Ezra Pound?"

"He was a very famous poet. Anyway, I don't think Ezra is necessarily the coolest name I've ever heard."

Hilda shrugged.

"Why do you like this guy?"

Hilda said, "I'm not sure. He seems to care, I guess. He cares that I am fat and that I have a bad name."

Max shook his head. "Hilda. You are not fat."

Hilda tried to swallow the sandy lump in her throat. "He thinks I should call myself Big H."

"Have you told him to change his name? Or I guess he already did. Ezra, my God."

"He also had this idea that I call myself Hot Dawg."

Max winced. "Hilda, the only thing you need to change is

your so-called boyfriend." He looked at her pale, sad face. "And get in touch with your inner H.D."

Hilda smiled. "Thanks," she said.

"I just wish I was that good with my own problems."

"Well, what would you say to you if you were me?"

He shrugged. "I'll have to think about that one."

He took the pink-and-silver bag she handed him and left the store. As he stepped out into the sunshine, he thought about Hilda's question.

Find the goddess inside yourself instead of looking for the god in someone else.

He wasn't sure if his advice was to Hilda, or to himself.

Sunset

Weetzie thought that Sunset Boulevard was the perfect Los Angeles street. It had a movie named after it. If you followed it from beginning to end, you would find most pieces of the city's puzzle. For Weetzie, the boulevard told a little story of her life. She had even been born on it.

It began near downtown, just after Chinatown with its cherry blossom–colored lanterns, its pagoda restaurants and stone dragons. Cesar Chavez Avenue—its sign printed in English, Spanish, and Chinese—changed into a boulevard called Sunset. This birth was marked by a sleazy motel called Paradise. What a perfect name, Weetzie thought. In a city that was partly paradise, or at least pretending to be paradise.

In Echo Park, there were sparse, dusty palm trees, tiny neighborhood markets selling meats and fruits, *panaderías, lavanderías*. There were clues that artists were hidden in the surrounding hills—a green building with headless mannequins and Day of the Dead skeletons on the balcony, bright murals defaced with graffiti, little outdoor cafés serving guava pastries and strong coffee.

At Alvarado, there was a sign announcing that this was part of the historic Route 66. Max once told Weetzie that it had been the main thoroughfare from Chicago before the Cold War, when Eisenhower built the interstate system, partly as an escape route in case of nuclear attack. Weetzie thought, Of course Max would have to bring nuclear attack into this. For her, Route 66 was just the song, full of finger-snapping cool and adventure. But there was something she loved about the fact that he knew things like that. Once she'd asked him why he couldn't just put them out of his mind, and he'd said, "It's the only way I know to take care of you."

In Silverlake, there was a Mexican restaurant strung with red chili pepper lights, a Spanish restaurant with flamenco dancers in the courtyard, and a bar called Akbar—after the fez-headed comic-strip character—in a triangular wedge of a building. Weetzie, Max, Dirk, and Duck spent many a happy happy hour drinking beers or having margaritas and chips on this part of the street. Every year they went to the Sunset Junction street fair to hear bands and eat greasy food. When Weetzie was very young, she had too many beers and ran around the fair with Dirk and a group of other people she couldn't remember, except for the odd-looking, skinny member of a seminal, now-defunct New Wave band who was gnawing on a giant, greasy turkey leg. "What a goat-rope this place is," he muttered when the rickety portable Ferris wheel they were riding got stuck in midair. The ornate, deco Vista Theatre stood on the corner where the street angled back around toward Hollywood.

Weetzie was born at Kaiser Hospital and went to Hollywood High School on Sunset. When she was little, her daddy took her to see *Mary Poppins* at the Cinerama Dome and he spent the whole second half of the movie chasing her in circles around the aisles. They liked to eat at the Old Spaghetti Factory, slurping up huge plates of noodles with marinara sauce in red-velvet Victorian train car seats. When Weetzie was older and Charlie moved to New York, she searched for someone to run through theaters and eat spaghetti with. She wore butterfly wings to the Palladium and stood alone in the darkness, listening to the band, hoping to find him. She played billiards next to rude eighties TV heartthrobs at the Hollywood Athletic Club. She drank martinis on the patio at the Cat and the Fiddle pub and ate cheap vegetarian Indian food at Paru's, but if he was there, too, he didn't recognize her. He did not discover her eating strawberry ice cream sundaes with marshmallow topping at Schwab's, but she did find her prom dress at the vintage clothing shop that opened up in its place, before that became the Virgin Megastore.

The Strip was lined with giant billboards. Weetzie saw a guy sleeping up on one once, in the eighties, staying there for as long as he could, to advertise something; she'd forgotten what. She remembered him, though, with his greasy eighties hair, handsome, grimy face, and cold eyes, joking with the crowd below. Doing anything to get some attention. That was what Sunset Boulevard was like. Big show-off street with its nightclubs blaring. Whiskey. Roxy. Rainbow. Starwood. Weetzie thought about all the bands she had seen here when she was young—the Weirdos, the Cramps, the Go-Go's, Oingo Boingo, Wall of Voodoo, the Unknowns, Suburban Lawns, the Adolescents, Fear, the Circle Jerks, the Screaming Sirens, Gears, X. Stepping into that world of music and darkness and smoke and beer, where you could forget who you were because you hadn't been it for that long anyway, where you could be a real artist, a stranger, dead movie star, broken doll, ghoul, gay boy, devil, princess, warrior, imagining you had found your muse, best friend, healer, beloved. Going home alone.

Just a few miles away, a palace belonging to a sheik had once been entirely surrounded by nude white statues with pubic hair painted on them. It was now just an ominous-looking black gate and a field of brown weeds. Everywhere else the street was lined with rolling green lawns, mansions, and signs advertising maps to stars' homes. Marlene Dietrich. Charlie Chaplin. Humphrey Bogart and Lauren Bacall. If you purchased one, you could even find the Brentwood apartment where Marilyn died.

The farther west you went, the more the street succumbed to nature. Clusters of happy palm trees decked with strands of their own pearls; banana trees; eucalyptus with peeling bark; white-blossoming magnolia; the odd exotic willow; fir and jacaranda; banks of ivy; and the pale blue flowers that Weetzie used to stick in her hair with their own juice. The trees had a secret; behind them were lovely homes or smaller streets leading to hidden parks and wild canyons. And then Sunset dipped down—past the lake shrine trimmed in azure and gold—down, down went the street, seeking the ocean like a lover—just as Weetzie would, tonight.

Ocean

Weetzie hadn't been able to sleep all night because of the sound of her heart—tick tock tick tock; she lay awake in her clothes, watching the clock. At eleven forty-five, she got up and went outside. The air had an odd scent, and she realized it was a salt sea breeze. She had never smelled the ocean from the pink hotel before.

Weetzie thought about the footsteps. She found herself half-wanting to hear them. Was it true what Charlie had said? That a part of Max was following her? But why hadn't he called her all this time? And what if she had dreamed the whole thing with Charlie? What if the footsteps were some-one else's? She jogged down the path, toward the main hotel.

It was very quiet there. Weetzie took the stairs to the top floor. When she got to the large suite at the end of the hall, she waited, not sure what to do next. Suddenly, the door opened and Shelley stepped out into the hallway. She was wearing a man's baseball cap with her hair tucked up inside and a baggy, dark sweatsuit. Her face looked pale and blurry, without any makeup to define it, and her eyes were red. She reached out her hand and Weetzie took it. They ran down the stairs, through the empty lobby, and into the night.

The T-bird roared along Sunset. Weetzie wanted to tell Shelley her stories about the street but it didn't seem like the right time. Shelley didn't say anything, still. Every once in a while, though, she would reach out, grab Weetzie's hand, and squeeze it so hard that it hurt.

Weetzie dropped down onto Pacific Coast Highway, took it for a ways, and then pulled into the parking lot of a small, ramshackle surf shop with morning glory vines growing over the low wooden roof and a hand-written sign that read DUCK'S. Shelley looked at her, questioning.

"Don't worry. I have a friend who will help us."

Duck Drake was waiting in his yellow VW Bug outside his shop just as he had promised when Weetzie called him that morning. He wore a faded orange, long-sleeved T-shirt, board shorts, and flip-flops. His blond hair was standing on end and his eyes were bleary.

"Hey, Weetz!"

"Duck, this is Shelley."

Duck kissed Shelley's hand, and she smiled for the first time. "Let's go, girls."

Weetzie and Shelley got in the VW. Duck put on a David Bowie CD. He and Weetzie sang along. " *'We can be heroes, just for one day . . .'* " They drove along the highway for a long time. Finally he turned off onto a dirt road, parked the car on the side of a slope above the sea, and got out. Shelley looked at Weetzie.

"Here?"

"No. We thought it would be better to take you somewhere more secluded."

"It's a hike," Duck said.

Shelley grabbed Weetzie's hand.

"It's okay. He knows. We'll help you."

The path wound down through brambles and sharp rocks. Shelley's feet slid on the dirt and gravel, so Duck and Weetzie held her between them, guiding her steps. Finally they reached Duck's favorite secret beach. The slopes were covered with Mexican evening primrose and California poppies. Instead of sand, shiny black stones glimmered in the moonlight. Clear water slithered up the shore as if it were trying to pull Shelley in, Weetzie thought. And the air was full of echoing voices, but that could have just been the surf breaking on the rocks.

Shelley took off her cap and shook out her long, greenish hair. Then she pulled off her clothes as if they had begun to itch her terribly, as if their weight was too much to bear a second longer. She stood naked on the beach with her Barbie doll body—gravity-defying breasts, tiny waist, and odd, stiff, doll legs and feet. Her eyes watched the ocean, unblinking. Then she turned and stroked her thumb against Weetzie's lips.

The mermaid made soft, gurgling music in her throat that echoed out toward the horizon. Before Weetzie could say anything, Shelley was stumbling over the black rocks. As soon as the water touched her feet, her whole body changed. She bent and immersed herself in the waves, wading out farther and farther, then leaping into the surf. Weetzie and Duck watched for a while, until they could no longer see her. Then Duck put his arm around Weetzie's shoulders.

"Thank you," she said. She wanted to close her eyes and go to sleep in his arms.

"Hey, it's nothing. But I hope you're coming home now, dude."

Weetzie looked out at the horizon where the sun would rise in a few hours, scalding the waves with light. By then, Shelley would be deep under the water. Maybe she was on her way to her mother. Weetzie knew she should be ready to go home now, but somehow she wasn't. She put her arm around Duck's warm, broad back.

"Not yet, dude," she said.

The End
of the Blues

Weetzie was so tired that she could feel the shape of her skull beneath her skin, her cheeks caving in, her eyes sinking deeper into their sockets. But the morning air was dewy and fresh, the sun was rising in the reflecting pool, and a flock of birds lifted off the lawn into the almost fluorescent sky.

The valet, whom Weetzie had come to think of as Rudy, opened her car door when she arrived back at the hotel. His jacket sleeve pulled up and she saw that his arm was covered with intricate tattoos. In that jungle of ink and skin, she thought she saw a red heart with MY SECRET written on it with thorns.

She stopped at the front desk to check for messages. The Blue Lady stepped out from behind the glossy leaves of a small potted lemon tree. She was smiling brightly.

"Good morning. May I help you?"

"How are you?"

"Fine, Ms. Bat, and you?"

Weetzie said, "Have you heard from your boyfriend?"

The woman looked surprised. "Excuse me?"

"I'm sorry. I was just curious. You seem so happy today."

"Not a word. But I really don't mind anymore. There are so many things to do and people to see." Then a secretive smile crossed her face. "I do think something has changed, though." Her eyes widened. "Maybe someone is coming."

Weetzie looked through the French doors into the garden. What appeared to be a large blue flower suddenly broke apart, its petals floating into the air. Weetzie realized it was not a flower at all, but a clustered flock of butterflies like the one she and Ping had seen. Who was coming? Weetzie wondered.

"Did I get any messages?" she asked.

The Blue Lady checked and shook her head. "I'm sorry. I don't see anything."

Weetzie felt a surprising sinking feeling. I'm just tired, she told herself. Why should I think Max would call now? Why do I want him to call? She thanked the Blue Lady and went outside.

As she stood beside the reflecting pool, gazing out over the lawn in the shadow of the pink hotel, something tickled her fingers and she looked down to see one of the large blue butterflies perched on her hand, wiggling its antennae at her.

Things That
Keep You Here

All that day, she slept. It was a deep, daytime sleep, thick
gauze wrapping her, like some kind of cocoon. When she
woke, she showered and then went to her closet to dress for
Heaven's ball.

Sometimes you fall, spinning through space, grasping for
the things that keep you on this earth. Sometimes you catch
them. They can be the hands of the people you love. They
can be your pets—pups with funny names, cats with ferocious old souls. The thing that keeps you here can be your
art. It can be things you have collected and invested with a
certain sense of meaning. A flowered, buckled treasure chest
of secrets. Shoes that make you taller and, therefore, closer
to the heavens. A suit that belonged to your fairy god-
mother. A dress that makes you feel a little like the Goddess
herself.

Sometimes you keep falling, you don't catch anything.

The night before, Weetzie had put all her clothes, except for Emilia, the pink sandals, and the clothes she had worn to take Shelley back to the sea, into the white case with the gold hardware and pink roses:

> *a handmade lime green, pink, and orange kimono-print string*
> *bikini*
> *five men's extra-small white tank tops from the surplus store*
> *white Levi's 501 jeans with a faint trace of a soy sauce stain*
> *men's black silk gabardine trousers from the Salvation Army,*
> *tailored to fit*
> *orange-leather, silver-studded slides*
> *some bikini underwear and bras in black, white, pink, and*
> *lime green*
> *a black silk-and-lace camisole*
> *a short, white satin designer trench*
> *a pair of high-heeled black ankle-strap sandals*
> *a black-leather, silver-studded belt from a 1980s hardcore*
> *punk store called Poseur*
> *a white satin hand-sewn minidress that bore a slight resem-*
> *blance to a toga*
> *a finely woven suit from Lacey's Beautiful World*
> *Coco*

The white case with pink roses and everything in it was gone. The pink sandals were gone. Emilia was gone.

Weetzie sat down on the floor and wept. As she cried, she

clutched the necklace of kisses around her neck. Why are you crying? she asked herself. You still have the necklace. These are only clothes. You didn't cry like this when you left Max, your secret agent lover man, the love of your life.

This made her cry even harder.

A Brief History of
Fashion, According
to Miss Weetzie Bat

1966: You insist on wearing only a green turtleneck and blue corduroy pants, much to your mother's dismay. You refuse the frilly pink dresses and pale blue suits with Peter Pan collars. Little does your mother know that in fifteen years you will wish you could dress like that every day (with combat boots or black stilettos, of course).

1973: You go to London with your mother and father. The girls are wearing miniskirts, tights, purple suede platform shoes. They have false eyelashes and shiny lips. The boutiques are filled with color and music. Your father buys you some purple suede gillies and you beg your mother to shorten all your dresses to the top of your thighs. You feel you have discovered fashion.

1974: You become obsessed with your mother's fashion magazines. You lie on your stomach pawing through them, touching the images. The designers are Yves Saint Laurent,

Karl Lagerfeld, Oscar de la Renta, Sonia Rykiel. You love the sound of their names. The models have feathered hair and wear chiffon peasant dresses covered with roses or sweater sets encrusted with jewels. In one magazine, the black-haired, blue-eyed model is photographed in the homes of the designers. The elegant men serve her wine, baguettes, and cheese, recline with her on their sofas and beds. She is their muse. You decide that a muse is what you want to be when you grow up.

1976: You go to junior high school wearing Ditto's jeans, Korkees sandals, and T-shirts you have adorned with rhinestones using a gun from an arts and crafts store. You have a Levi's jacket that you cover with appliqués of butterflies. The prettiest girl in your class, Corinne Nichols, admires your jacket. You make her one. She only wears it once but it makes you feel popular and special. She appears in *Seventeen* magazine. You imagine that instead of being a muse you will grow up to be a designer. You sew a pink wraparound skirt and a voile blouse with fairies on it. You buy T-shirts, cut them, and sew laces up the front. You adorn them with tiny silk roses and dye them pastel colors. Some of the popular girls ask you to make them one. At the end of the school year, Corinne Nichols writes in your yearbook in round cursive letters, "Thank you for the pretty jacket." You imagine that you, too, are popular.

1977: How unfortunate that just as you are trying to develop breasts, tube tops come into fashion. Mortifying, actually. You cannot comprehend why anyone would want to wear a band of stretchy elastic over her boobs. These things show everything and can be pulled off with one tug! Yuck.

1978: You are not happy about the disco trend. It's better than tube tops but still makes you uncomfortable and embarrassed. You go to a few dance clubs wearing spandex pants, Candie's slides, and shirts with double belts. You wish you had been born in a different era. Ten years ago you would have made a perfect flower child, part of a movement!

1980: The popular girls do not invite you to their parties. You spend time alone, sewing, listening to music, rollerskating around the city. There is a boy in school with a Mohawk. He wears black pants with chains, and steel boots, and ripped T-shirts. You've never seen anyone like him. You buy some punk albums at the record store. You feel you have discovered music. You go to your first punk rock show. You come home and take everything out of your closet. You rip up all of your T-shirts. You throw away your pastel jeans. You keep only your Levi's 501s, which you wash as often as possible, hoping they will get holes in them. You stop reading your fashion magazines. You go to all the thrift stores you can find. With just a few dollars, you buy a pair of engineer boots with steel toes, a small black-leather motorcycle jacket, a pleated red plaid miniskirt, and armloads of old silk dresses that no one seems to want. You feel that you have discovered the true meaning of fashion. You raid your mother's closet for rhinestone jewelry, beaded sweaters, miniskirts, and pointed pumps. You go to the surplus store for boys' T-shirts that you rip up and adorn with safety pins. You cut off all your hair and bleach it platinum. You decide to talk to the boy with the Mohawk, whose name is Dirk.

1981: Dirk's Grandmother Fifi dies. She leaves you her

clothes—gowns, suits, hats, shoes. A genuine Chanel. A Pucci. You read about Coco and how Marilyn loved Emilio. You think that the Pucci prints are like highly magnified pictures of the inner workings of nature. These clothes transform you. They are like magic. Your treasures.

1982: You shop on Melrose. There are stores called Vertigo and Neo80 and Wacko and Tiger Rose. Cowboys and Poodles has fifties clothes that have never been worn before. Gräu is owned by a designer with feral eyes who sits in front of an aqua vinyl curtain by a bowl of gardenias, sewing "depression wear." Let It Rock features rocker clothes from London, including electric-blue suede "creepers" with big black rubber soles and a pink-leather motorcycle jacket that you save up for and buy. You wear the motorcycle jacket with a glittery tutu. You feel as if you are finally part of some kind of movement.

1986: Melrose is now rows of cheap, sexy, stretchy clothes. The artists move east. You stay home, happily sewing dresses covered with pacifiers, jackets made of teddy bears, pants of white silk flowers, elaborate, sparkly costumes for your daughters. They become your muses.

1992: You realize that you have spent the last few years in mom clothes—capri pants or jeans, flip-flops or sneakers, and tank tops—only dressing up with style when you go out at night or play a part in a movie. You look at fashion magazines again, but you are not impressed or inspired. The designers seem somehow cold and mean-spirited. You dream of having your own store.

1995: The nineties confuse you. You recall that it began

with Madonna in a bra with sharp gold cones. Somehow this was one Madonna look you were not able to embrace. You spend most of your time wearing fitted, black clothes. You see an exhibition of a female Japanese artist's work at the Los Angeles County Museum. There is a dress made of white iron, covered with delicate, intricate wrought-iron flowers. You believe it is the perfect metaphor for fashion.

1998: Kabbalah. Yoga. Frida Kahlo. The Goddess is coming out of hiding. You decide that you love clothing again. You can't read enough fashion magazines. You go to cheap stores by the beach and buy Asian-print tops covered with rhinestones that you wear with jeans, and bejeweled skirts that you wear with flip-flops and T-shirts. You buy sheer, sequin-embroidered saris at the Indian shop and make them into tops and scarves. You cut up old kimonos and piano shawls and make them into jackets. You are a new bohemian. You open your store. When you walk through the French doors, you feel you are in your own little altar to the Goddess.

2001: You are depressed about getting older. You watch *Hedwig and the Angry Inch*. When beautiful Hedwig's lover reacts in horror to her naked body, Hedwig tells him, "It's what I've got to work with." Work it she does. You decide to do the same! Feeling that you have proven yourself in the trenches of thrift-shopping, hand-sewing, and bargain-hunting, you buy a white satin trench coat by a hot young designer. It costs more than you have ever spent on anything, but you feel that, finally, you deserve it. You also buy designer stilettos in black and a white bag. You tell yourself they are classics; you will have them forever.

Events happen in the world that make you recognize the impermanence of everything. You realize that forever is not what it seems. This only helps you justify your purchases more.

2003: Your most treasured items of clothing are stolen. You try to decide if you should take this as a message of endings. Or beginnings.

Prom Night

Weetzie Bat went alone to Heaven's ball. She wore a white tank top, orange cropped and zippered pants, and orange sneakers, stained from sand and mud. Around her neck she wore the necklace of kisses.

On the way to the room in the hotel where she had attended her high school prom, Weetzie saw a large white animal. At first she thought he was a small horse. His legs were balletic, almost as long as hers. His head was noble and heavy, like a marble sculpture.

"Hey, fella," Weetzie said. "Hey, beautiful. Will you be my date?"

The Great Dane pushed the top of his head against the palm of her hand. His skull felt so smooth. There was something almost prehistoric about him. He looked up at her with eyes like Quan Yin, the Chinese goddess of compassion.

Weetzie and her companion walked together into the

hotel. No one stopped to question her about him. He was not really like a dog, after all. He was otherworldly, like the pink hotel.

On the second floor, a large pair of doors opened into the room with the pink-and-green parquet dance floor surrounded by tables covered with white linen tablecloths and pink-and-white stargazer lilies. Hundreds and hundreds of white balloons and an endless stream of soap bubbles hovered around a mirrored disco ball on the ceiling. There was an ice cream sundae cart, a cappuccino cart, a clown making animal balloons, and another clown painting people's faces. The Boom Band was playing on a low stage in the back, and the guests were dancing to their hypnotic music with wild abandon. Some were doing cartwheels and handsprings around the dance floor. They were dressed for proms and for their own weddings and for every party they had ever dreamed of attending and not been invited to attend. The twelve sisters in damask gowns and beaded flats whirled past. Weetzie looked down at her soiled clothes and sneakers.

The white-haired woman from the wedding came over and took Weetzie's hand.

"May I have this dance, my dear?"

Weetzie said, "I'm not really dressed . . ."

The woman ignored her and led her out onto the floor. The music took over and Weetzie whirled with her, forgetting everything. When the dance ended, the woman took Weetzie aside.

"Did you find your animus?"

"I saw him," Weetzie said. "But he wasn't what I thought he'd be."

"What's that?"

"I don't know. The perfect lover. He wasn't interested in me at all."

"Is that the point?"

"What do you mean?"

"Your animus isn't supposed to be interested in you. He's supposed to be integrated into you. That way you won't go chasing some idealized dream lover the rest of your days."

Weetzie looked around the dance floor. The gamine bride and the tall, beaky groom from the wedding breezed past her. Their faces were painted white and they wore small white skullcaps and matching white silk suits with huge buttons and collars. The bride had rosettes on her slippers. Weetzie thought she saw the couple levitate a few inches off the floor.

"Ah, honeymoon," the white-haired woman said. "Isn't that the loveliest word?"

Honey. Moon. Weetzie thought it was as good as "numinous." She wished she had had one of her own. Maybe the stay at the pink hotel counted as a solo version.

"Sweetheart, are you all right?" It was Heaven, dressed in a ruby red ball gown. She held Weetzie at arm's length and surveyed her dirty clothes. "You look like you've been cleaning out the ashes. Where's your ball gown, Cinderella?"

Weetzie said, "I wasn't planning on wearing this."

"I imagine not. You'd be better off in the nude. We could attach a centerpiece between your legs." She gestured to the stargazer lilies on the tables.

"I was going to wear . . ."

Before she could finish, Weetzie saw a young woman parade past her on the arm of a white-haired man.

"That!" Weetzie said. The woman was wearing Emilia and the raspberry pink sandals.

Before she knew it, Weetzie was being dragged onto the dance floor. Sal pulled her close and hissed in her ear.

"I had the strangest thing happen to me this morning. I woke all tied up in the biggest, strongest spiderweb I've ever seen. It took all day to get out of it."

Weetzie tried not to look away. His breath smelled of liquor and his eyes were bloodshot. She felt his fingers digging into her arm.

"Your friend is wearing my Pucci," Weetzie said. "And my shoes."

"Well, well," said Sal. "Isn't that funny. Tit for tat. Or, in this case, tat for tit. I guess we traded possessions. I can live without mine. Can you?"

He dropped her arm as if he were tossing something into a trashcan and walked away. Weetzie steadied herself.

"What was that about?" Heaven asked.

"I think he stole some of my clothes," she said softly. She put her hand on Heaven's arm as she started after Sal. "But he's right in a way. I guess we're even."

"Are you sure?"

Weetzie nodded and watched, wistfully, as Emilia left the ballroom.

"Well, let me know if you change your mind!" Heaven kissed her and danced off.

Weetzie heard her name. Dashell Hart and Tristan Sable were seated with Pan and a very young woman wearing a short, diaphanous, pleated column of a dress and a crown of gold leaves on her tousled dark hair. Weetzie went to greet them. They all got up and kissed her cheek, except for the woman, who only stared.

"This is Phaedra," Dashell said. "She plays a nymph on the show."

"Hi, Phaedra."

The dark-haired woman managed a small smile and put her hand on Pan's bicep.

That was quick, thought Weetzie, but after all, they were at the pink hotel. She hoped that Pan and Phaedra would be very happy laughing, crying, and coming together.

The honeymooners, in their commedia del'arte costumes, floated by, pressed chest to chest a few inches off the ground. Pan got up and took Phaedra's hand. Tristan Sable was led onto the floor by the white-haired woman. Heaven found Dashell Hart. Weetzie watched them. She felt a pain in her chest as if her heart were a glass disco ball that had been smashed into thousands of little pieces.

The twelve princesses danced by.

"Come join us!" they called. "Girls just want to have fun! Come dance with us! You never have to stop dancing!"

Weetzie said, "Thanks, ladies, but I can't. Then there would be thirteen of us."

They ignored her and two of them took her hands. Soon she was dancing by herself, in the midst of the twelve damask dresses, whirling like a dervish. Sweat poured off her body like tears. Her heart pounded in her chest; it had not broken after all.

An hour later, Weetzie was still dancing. She spun so fast, the room was a carousel. Losing her balance, she went reeling.

Sometimes you fall, spinning through space, grasping for the things that keep you here. Sometimes you catch them. Sometimes you don't.

Sometimes they catch you.

Weetzie careened into a man in a tuxedo standing at the entrance to the ballroom.

It was Max.

When their bodies touched, the lights in the ballroom flickered for a moment. There was a slight shifting of earth beneath the pink hotel. The chandeliers tinkled. Balloons burst, sprinkling confetti over the dancers. Champagne corks popped. A swarm of blue butterflies flew through the open windows.

Weetzie felt something cold and wet pressing against her leg. It was the white dog's nose. He stood there, watching her, swaying his head from side to side. Then he turned and high-stepped out the door.

Max and Weetzie followed him down the staircase, through the lobby, into the garden.

The Necklace
of Kisses

The moon was completely full, white and papery like a lantern. It was so bright that the birds sang, believing morning had come. Weetzie and Max followed the white dog across a little bridge over a stream and into a grotto of moss and vines. The air smelled of American Beauties, Marilyns, and Sugar Plum Fairy roses. Max handed Weetzie a large silver box swathed in sheer pink tulle. She unwrapped it and took out the pink gloves, the gold shoes, and the dress.

"Princess Grace!" she said.

Max smiled. Weetzie looked into his tired, green eyes. She used her toe to push off one orange sneaker, and then the other. She wriggled out of her tank top, unfastened her orange pants, and let them fall off her hips to the ground. She wedged her rather sweaty, swollen feet into the golden shoes. She slid the long pink satin gloves up to her elbows, smoothed them out, and buttoned the pearl buttons.

Then she reached behind herself and unhooked her orange bra. She slowly slid off her orange panties. Max had seen her naked before so many times. There in the moonlight, in the garden of the pink hotel, it felt like the first.

Weetzie stepped into the huge tulle skirt covered with roses, careful not to catch it on the spikes of her heels. She leaned forward and shimmied her breasts into the cups of the dress, the way she had seen her mother do when she was young. Arms akimbo, she tried to find the zipper but couldn't. Max put his hands on her waist and gently, firmly, turned her around. He lightly grazed her skin with the zipper before it slid up smoothly. She shivered from the slight pain as she turned back to face him again.

Max put both his hands on Weetzie's throat, touching the necklace of kisses. His fingers were warm and dry, trembling slightly. Weetzie helped Max take off his tuxedo jacket and bow tie and unbuttoned the collar of his white shirt. She could see the pulse in his neck. She reached up to her own and undid the tiny catch with her thumbnail. Then Weetzie Bat fastened the necklace of kisses around her secret agent lover man's throat.

Waking from his two-year-long September, he pressed his lips to hers.

This is what happened:

Daisy Montgomery, who would never have her wedding night in the pink hotel, lifted out of the mist above the reflecting pool and flew off into the night sky.

The sleeping goddess statues that the madam's son had hidden in the garden opened their eyes.

Keiko Yamaguchi, the former owner of the pink hotel, who was now working secretly as a waitress in the Japanese restaurant, woke suddenly in her room, stumbled to the mirror, and saw that the hormones she had been taking for months, to no effect, had started to work.

Isis Kenna Clay, the hotel receptionist, woke suddenly in her courtyard bungalow in West Hollywood, yawned, rubbed her face with her palms, stumbled to the bathroom, looked in the mirror, and found that her skin was no longer blue, but its original shade—a deep, rich ebony.

In the ballroom, Dashell Hart turned to the young actor Pan and offered him a role in the soap opera *Eden Place.*

Tristan Sable peered into the pocket of his tuxedo, where he discovered his long-lost friend Stem hiding.

The twin masseurs' father, Bear, a burly Swiss man with a long, white beard, entered the ballroom. The white-haired woman, recognizing her future husband, smiled to herself and went to ask him for a dance.

After a day and night of traveling, the artist walked into the white, wood-frame house in Upstate New York. He could hear the brook that ran through the backyard and see the shadow of the willow tree on the wall.

Then Zane Starling went upstairs to the large bed, where his wife was sleeping on fresh white linens with his two youngest children. She opened her eyes when she felt his breath on her face. The look she gave him was one he had seen six times before, so he did not need her to use words to tell him—she was pregnant again.

Somewhere in the Pacific Ocean, a mermaid with the legs of a woman swam in a school of dolphins to a cave covered with barnacles. The dolphins whistled good-bye and surged off. The mermaid went into the cave and found her mother sleeping there in a pile of the pearls she had wept.

Somewhere in a graveyard in New Orleans, three strange-looking people with red hair and an empty baby carriage were struck with amnesia. They stopped in their tracks and stared at each other, wondering why the hell they had come here in the first place.

Esmeralda Escobar woke suddenly in her apartment near downtown Los Angeles and grabbed her sleeping husband's shoulders. *"Mira!"* she said. He opened his eyes and rubbed them three times to make sure he was not dreaming when he saw the girl he had married, grown older now, sitting beside him, her horse's mane of black hair loose around her shoulders.

Dirk McDonald and Duck Drake had the same dream: Weet-zie had come home. She was standing on the doorstep, naked and laughing. They rolled over in bed, found each other, and made love in their canyon house of cherry wood and stained-glass windows.

Ping Chong Jah-Love felt something fluttering against her face. She woke to see two huge, fluorescent-blue butterflies in her bedroom. The pair circled for a while and then landed on sleeping Valentine Jah-Love's big, bare shoulder, where they began to mate delicately. Ping did not take this as a sign of global warming, or any other planetary distress, but as a sure message that Weetzie and Max had found each other again.

In Santa Barbara, Cherokee Bat woke suddenly, sat at the sewing machine in the shape of a sphinx, and began to work. She was making a sleeveless cream-silk sheath over slim, sheer cream-chiffon pants and a cream raw-silk three-quarter-length coat with a pale blue lining covered with silver stars. In the lining, she would put tiny notes, little charms to honor and protect the enchantress, her mother.

In a café on Telegraph Avenue, Witch Baby sat across the table from her beloved Angel Juan and said, "What were you looking for?"

"You," he answered.

"But you didn't know it?"

"Not until now."

She nodded. She said, "Now I need to find what I am looking for."

Hilda Doolittle sat at her desk in her one-room Echo Park apartment, looking out over Sunset Boulevard through a window hung with skeleton lights. She was writing a poem called "The Goddess in You." On the wall, she saw the unmistakable shadow of a woman, though there was no one there but herself.

A young starlet left the hotel room of the producer with whom she had spent the evening and who was now asleep on the couch. She was carrying a white case covered with roses. She drove away from the pink hotel, never to return. As she merged onto the freeway, her car trunk popped open, the latch on the white case undid itself, and a pink-and-green silk dress flew off into the night sky.

While everyone in the ballroom kissed each other, Heaven stepped onto the balcony. As soon as the moonlight touched Heaven, Haven emerged.

"We need to send her some CDs," said Haven. "She's still talking about 'Seasons in the Sun.'"

Heaven rolled her eyes. They took each other's hands and looked out over the grounds of the pink hotel.

"What a strange and beautiful night," Heaven sighed.

All of the little atrium shops were dark. Except for one.

In her Beautiful World, Lacey was weaving a tapestry, telling a story out of her body. It was about people on fire. It was about people in love. It was about people falling from burning buildings. It was about people discovering they could fly.